Mystery a

'There was a m[...]
house. Out towards the west there was an
unbroken view for several miles over rolling
fields dotted with little white farm-houses. On
a clear day they could even make out the shape
of cottages on the lower slopes of Nephin. To
the south they could see the clump of hazel and
hawthorn which marked their own ring fort,
and beyond that the expanse, at present
spotted with cocks of new-made hay, of the
Rinn Mór which gave the village its name.'
The children are looking forward to a long
lazy summer. But, suddenly, there is a
dramatic development . . .

Jo Ann Galligan

Mystery at Rinn Mór

Illustrated by Terry Myler

ACORN BOOKS
The Children's Press

To my father,
Claude Belgrave,
late RNZN Lieutenant

First published in 1985 by
The Children's Press
90 Lower Baggot Street, Dublin 2

© Text: Jo Ann Galligan
© Illustrations: The Children's Press

This book is published with the financial
assistance of the Arts Council
(An Chomhairle Ealaíon), Dublin

ISBN 0 900068 95 7 cased
ISBN 0 900068 96 5 paper

Typesetting by Computertype Limited
Printed in Ireland by Mount Salus Press Limited

Contents

1 Liam

From his perch in the old sycamore, Kevin McDonagh could just see the men loading up their vans down on the Swinford Road.

'The travellers are moving out,' he said. 'Must be going somewhere else for the summer. Just imagine, they could be heading for the seaside!'

Maureen poked her head out between two branches, shaking her dark plaits free of the smaller twigs. 'Wouldn't mind going to the seaside myself. It's warm enough today for a swim!'

'I wonder what it's like living in a caravan?' said Kevin. 'I think I'd like to try sometime.'

'Tree-houses are better,' said Teddy. 'You can sit up here all day and watch everyone and no one knows where you are! One day I'm going to put a proper roof on — then we'll stay out here all night!'

'Mum wouldn't let us,' protested Kevin.

'Wouldn't let *you*, you mean! You're only a baby. She'd let us big ones stay here, wouldn't she, Maureen?'

'She might. I'm not sure I'd like to,' grinned Maureen. 'You snore!'

Teddy, smirking back at her, shouted, 'And you talk in your sleep,' before swinging himself out of reach into the higher branches. Maureen, a year older and slightly heavier, didn't follow him in case a branch broke. As the eldest, she felt she had to strike a responsible note.

'Stop it, you two,' ordered Kevin. 'You're shaking the

whole tree-house. What's the point of having a nice private place if you make all that noise? All the kids in the village will hear us and know we're up here!'

'I built it,' said Teddy. 'I'm the one who says what we do up here.'

Maureen made a face at him and sat back against the railing, concentrating on a rider a few fields away. He was having trouble controlling his pony, and Maureen, who was interested in animals of all kinds and hoped one day to be a vet, followed his actions with interest. The rider appeared to be bare-back, trusting to a loose bridle and his own knees to guide the animal.

Seeing that Maureen was not going to argue any more, Teddy came back down to the platform and surveyed his work. He had finished only the previous day, after the last of the hay had been cocked, and was proud of his first 'house'. Several old planks had been lashed together across the bole of the tree to form a platform, then he had nailed some smaller planks along three sides to form a combined safety-rail and screen from inquisitive eyes. The fourth side and 'roof' were made of old leafy branches, pruned from the many alders along the roadsides. When the children were on the platform and had drawn the branches over themselves they were in a little world of their own and no one could see them, not even their parents.

There was a marvellous view from the tree-house, and this was one of the reasons why Teddy had chosen this tree. Out towards the west there was an unbroken view for several miles over rolling fields dotted with little white farmhouses. On a clear day they could even make out the shapes of cottages on the lower slopes of

Nephin. To the south they could see the clump of hazel and hawthorn which marked their own ring fort, and beyond that the expanse, at present spotted with cocks of new-made hay, of the Rinn Mór which gave the village its name. Kevin's little kitchen garden was immediately below them, with the main Swinford road running beyond their own boreen, and to their east was the gable wall of the house. Teddy planned to spend many days up here, adding a proper roof when his father had some offcuts to spare, and perhaps extending the platform out from the tree to give more area. Heights held no fear for him, and once he had decided to do something nothing could stop him.

Maureen who was still watching the pony and rider suddenly called, 'Look out! He's fallen off!'

The other two children turned to look in that direction. Then they all clambered down as fast as they could. Maureen was the first down and went jumping over the low stone wall and across the next field at top speed. Teddy was only a few paces behind her by the time he reached the far ditch, but Kevin had been left still clambering over the first wall.

'Are you all right?' gasped Maureen, trying to catch her breath and talk all at the same time.

The figure on the ground stirred, then rolled over to stare at her. 'I ... I think so.'

'What happened?' shouted Teddy, leaping down from the stones and dislodging several in his haste. 'Are you hurt?'

The boy rose to his feet, cautiously stretched one leg and then the other, and shook his mop of unruly red curls.

'I'm not hurt, just shaken. Where's the pony?'

'She's gone over the back fields. We'll catch her there; there's no way out.'

The boy rubbed his head. 'Cracked my skull, I think. There's a big bump here.'

Teddy ran his hand over it. 'There's a bump all right but no blood. You'll be all right. Who are you anyway? Do you live around here?'

'My name's Liam O'Connor,' answered the boy. 'I've got a job with Dan Moore. He broke his leg a few days ago and as I was already helping out with the haymaking and turf I decided to stay on with him for the summer. My family moved out today but he's paying me and giving me my keep and I'll be working with his ponies. That's his new pony I was riding. I've got the job of breaking her in.'

'Looks to me like she's breaking *you* in,' laughed Maureen. 'Do you belong to the travellers then?'

'Yes' said Liam. 'Dad trades in horses at the fairs, that's how I know how to handle them. My folks will be back in the autumn and I'll join up with them again.'

'Aren't you too young to be on your own?' asked Teddy. 'You're only a kid.'

'I'm fourteen,' retorted Liam. 'Besides, I'm not on my own. I'm staying with Dan Moore. And, anyway, if I'm big enough to have a job, I'm big enough to be on my own, aren't I? And who are you to talk? You're only babies!'

'I'm twelve,' said Maureen, 'and Teddy's eleven ... even if he's a bit small. We're no babies.'

'And I'm nine ... and nearly as tall as Teddy,' said Kevin, anxious not to be left out.

'Good!' Liam sounded slightly amused. 'Now, we've a pony to round up. I'll need some help'.

'It's down there,' said Maureen, pointing, 'I could see it from the top of the field. It's gone down the back of the Rinn, and as there are no low walls there it can't get out. We can coax it into a corner.'

'Let's go then,' said Liam. 'I don't want to lose her the first time I take her out. Come on, you can all help me.'

The four children crossed the two fields again and stopped at the near side of the Rinn to see what the pony was doing. She was grazing quietly in the far corner and appeared to have calmed down.

'I'll go round the ditch behind her,' said Liam. 'You spread out and walk down slowly, then try to drive her towards me. I have a spare rope here round my waist ... I can catch her with it.'

'I'll follow you on the inside of the ditch,' offered Maureen. 'She'll come to me.'

'She's right,' said Kevin. 'Maureen is very good with animals.'

'Good enough. No noise now, she's very nervous.'

Liam leapt easily over the stone wall and went loping down the field as silently as a cat. Maureen followed on the near side, wishing she had changed her footwear. She had been wearing runners in the tree-house and they were not really suitable for walking through the fields. It had rained after they cocked the hay and the ground was muddy in places.

The pony pricked up her ears twice but then returned to the young grass. All around her were cocks of fresh hay but she had ignored them and gone straight to the lush young grass at the side of the stone wall. The tractor had not been able to cut the very edges of the field and these leavings were always a welcome titbit for the McDonaghs' few cattle after the hay was all in and the aftergrass sprouting. Last year the field had been reseeded after a crop of oats so the grass was extra sweet and fine.

'Come, come, come, come,' whispered Maureen softly. Once more the pony lifted her head. This time

she caught sight of Maureen. The girl stood absolutely still, only blowing sharply down her nostrils. The pony gave a faint whinny, then paused. Maureen took two cautious steps forward, breathing out once more. The pony blew her own breath back then, and slowly they advanced towards each other, each offering her scent to the other. Then Maureen had one hand on the pony's neck and was scratching her and talking quietly. Immediately Liam was over the ditch and had the rope secured to the bridle, but this time the pony stood for him.

'Well done,' he said. 'You do know how to manage animals, don't you?'

'I want to be a vet,' confessed Maureen. 'I've always got on well with animals.'

'Well, Rascal here is a bit of a handful, aren't you, girl?'

Rascal shook her head and made to stamp with her hoof.

'No you don't,' said Maureen in the same soothing voice, and Rascal stood quietly again. 'Come on.' She took the rope from Liam and led the pony up the field towards the boys. Teddy swung the gate open and they all came through to the small field again. Maureen tied the rope to the gate.

'There you are,' she said. 'You can have a bit of the grass in here. If we leave you in the other field with the hay you might do some damage! I'm surprised you didn't have some!'

'She probably would have done if we hadn't moved her,' said Liam. 'I'm going to sit here and have a rest for a few minutes. My head is really sore.'

The three McDonagh children sat down beside him.

'No hurry anyway,' said Teddy, removing a wisp of hay from his blond hair and chewing on the end of it. 'We've got another eight weeks off school.'

'Not that we have much of a holiday,' objected Kevin. 'We were cocking hay all last week. Now we're off to the bog to turn the turf. It's all work!'

'Do you have to cut the turf yourselves?' asked Liam.

'No, the machine comes in and cuts it,' said Teddy. 'But this year has been so wet it's taken all this time to dry out. Dad says it's ready for turning now. Then next week, if the weather stays good, we have to foot it ready for bringing out to the road. We'll be over to borrow Dan's donkey and cart for that ... he lets us have it every year.'

'Some of Dan's turf is already out,' said Liam. 'We brought a couple of clamps out to the road last week, stuff that was made last year and not moved. Then we cut some more by slane but that won't be ready to touch for a while. So I guess he won't be needing the donkey for some time.'

'Good,' said Teddy. 'Some years we both need it at the same time, and then we have to wait.'

'Is it you that sells eggs to Dan?' asked Liam. 'He was talking about going to some neighbour this week to pick up some eggs. He says the shop eggs are no good!'

'Course they're not!' Teddy agreed, grinning. 'Yes, I'm the egg neighbour! That's my job on the farm. When I'm not helping Dad with his carpentry, I have my hens to see to. I've got three dozen, and I sell eggs to a couple of the people around.'

'I'll be over to pick some up one day, so.'

14

'I'll keep the freshest,' offered Teddy. 'Not that you could call them anything else. I never have an egg around that's older than a couple of days. What we don't sell, we eat!'

'He's only boasting,' said Maureen. 'We all have jobs to do. I milk our cow and feed her calf, and Kevin grows lettuce and things for salad in the small garden by the tree ...'

Teddy kicked her hard and she choked over the last word. The tree-house was a secret and he did not intend any other children to know about it — not until he knew them a lot better!

'What I was going to say,' went on Maureen, glaring at Teddy and rubbing her leg where he had kicked her, 'was that Kevin's garden is by the big old sycamore in the garden near the west mairn.'

'This fort behind us,' said Liam, changing the subject, 'is this on your land, too?'

'Oh, yes,' said Teddy. 'The Rinn Mór is ours. It used to be common land but our family bought it through the Land Commission years ago. Then we have this field and the one beside it — you can see the fort is actually in the corners of two different fields — and then the house down there is in a third field, and there is another small field beside it. The rest of our land is across the boreen, opposite the house.'

'Is it as big as Dan's farm?' asked Liam.

'No way,' said Kevin. 'Ours is just a small-holding, not really a farm at all. Dan has a big place ... must be fifty acres. He bought a couple of strips next to his own land some years back and started raising horses along with the cattle.'

'Ponies,' corrected Liam. 'He has ponies. And the donkey of course.'

'All the same thing,' said Kevin. 'You can have a ride on any of them!'

'Take no notice,' said Maureen. 'He's not very interested in animals, apart from that dog of his. All he cares about is reading. He doesn't even know how to milk a cow!'

'I do so,' objected Kevin. 'I can't help it if my hands aren't big enough yet, can I?'

A voice from the house below interrupted them.

'Hey, that's Mum,' said Teddy. 'It must be dinnertime already. Are you going to ride back, Liam?'

'No, I think it would be better to lead her. I'll try riding her again tomorrow when she has had time to forget about throwing me off today!'

The voice came floating up the field again: 'Teddy, Maureen! Where are you all? The dinner's on the table and not one of you here to eat it!'

'Coming!' screamed Teddy, in a tone so shrill that Rascal started.

'Watch out, Teddy!' said Maureen. 'Don't spook her again!'

Liam slipped the rope off the gate and Maureen went around the other side. 'I'll walk her,' she said. 'Rascal will do what I tell her!'

True enough, Rascal turned her head towards her new friend and blew hard on Maureen's forehead.

'See?' she said. 'Rascal likes me. I think she ought to stay here with me!'

The two younger boys ran on ahead but she escorted Liam and the pony past the house and down towards the

16

gate. As they reached the outhouses a streak of yellow bounded out to meet them, circled them twice, then raced back at top speed to join Kevin.

'What was *that*?' asked Liam, casting a nervous glance at Rascal. It would not do for her to be frightened again.

'Oh, that's only Carrots. He's Kevin's dog, and the craziest dog you ever saw. He's all bounce and no bite.'

'That's a funny name for a dog. Why did you call him Carrots?'

'Well, we got him as a puppy, and it was winter so Mum said he could sleep in the kitchen the first few nights as it was so cold in the shed. When we all got up the next morning he had pulled all the carrots out of a bucket under the sink and chewed every one of them into little pieces. It wouldn't have been so bad if he had actually eaten the pieces, but after he had finished with the carrots he had eaten one of Dad's slippers and the strap of Teddy's schoolbag! That, and the colour of his coat, of course, is the reason he was called Carrots!'

'You're right!' laughed Liam. 'Fits him to a T! Now I'd better be off ... but I'll be back one of the days for some of Teddy's eggs.'

'Maybe you'll ride Rascal next time?' suggested Maureen. 'Can I have a ride next time too?'

'If she's quiet,' agreed Liam. 'She's okay right now but that will only last until she feels the weight on her back. Then she'll be frisky enough!'

'Maureen!' came her mother's voice once again.

'Coming!' called Maureen and began running back up to the house. Meanwhile Rascal and Liam set off briskly in the opposite direction.

2 The Stolen Cross

Although the day was warm, the McDonagh kitchen was cool and fresh. The big stove which kept the house so warm in winter was kept barely alight after dinner was cooked these summer days. It was pleasant to sit there after they had finished eating and relax, knowing that the hay — always the most frantic of the summer jobs — was saved.

'More tea?' asked Eileen McDonagh, turning back to the table. 'There's plenty in the pot here.'

'I'll have some more,' agreed her husband, holding up his cup.

'Watch out, Dad!' shouted Kevin. 'You're going to spill it. That paper must be really interesting. You haven't stopped reading it since you finished eating.'

'Kevin's right,' said Eileen. 'You're going to spill that drop if you don't stop waving it about. Now, put that paper down and give me that cup here, Con, if you want some more in it.'

'What's so interesting anyway, Dad?' asked Teddy, as his father folded the paper and put it on the chair behind him. 'Have we won that competition?'

'I don't know anything about any competition,' replied Con. 'I was reading about the cross that was stolen.'

Eileen, teapot in hand, paused beside the cup. 'What cross is that? There was nothing on the radio.'

'You must have missed it then. It's the biggest story

of the day. You know that cross they excavated a few years ago in Westport? It's supposed to date from the time of St. Patrick.'

'You mean that Westport gold find?' asked Maureen.

'That's it. There were several pieces in what appeared to be an old grave. They think that a monk was buried there at one time, and later on for some reason the body was removed and reburied somewhere else. However the gold was left in the original grave, probably for safety, or perhaps when the exhumation took place nobody realised that it was there at all. There could have been rubble between the gold and the monk's body, and if nobody knew it was there they would not have bothered to dig any further.

'However, it came about that the gold was left there, and it was rediscovered only a few years ago when they were bulldozing a hillside to make way for a new housing estate. When the grave was uncovered, work stopped and archaeologists had to be sent for to examine the find. It was nearly a month before everything was photographed and itemized and the council could start work again.'

'What happened to the gold that was found?' asked Kevin.

'It was all sent down to the museum in Dublin. The cross from the collection, which is supposed to be a really beautiful piece of work and the most valuable of all, has been on loan to Westport House these last few weeks. The museum curator from Dublin and his assistant were apparently travelling by car to bring it back in person.'

'And what happened?' inquired Teddy hopefully.

19

'Was somebody murdered?'

'Don't be so dramatic,' cautioned his father. 'Of course not. The cross was stolen, that's all.'

'Who stole it?' asked Maureen.

'All we know is that three men were involved. The driver bringing the curator back to Dublin turned out to be an impersonator. The real driver was found, tied up and gagged, in his own garage. Meanwhile, the curator and his companion were found tied to the seats of their car in the grounds of the community centre here. Some youngsters on their way in for sports practice heard grunts and when they investigated and found the two men, they set them free and then called the guards. The men were unharmed — but the blue case with the cross in it had gone. The men had been prisoners for a couple of hours so the thieves had a bit of a headstart. However we don't know whether or not they had a getaway car arranged. The boys who rescued them didn't notice any strangers around, and of course the two men were well tied so they were unable to swivel round to see what was going on.'

'So the cross could still be in this area,' said Maureen. 'Have the police started looking for it?'

'They have been stopping all cars leaving the Swinford area, but the thieves may have got away before their captives were discovered. It seems fairly likely to me that they did have a car waiting, or were planning to steal one after leaving the centre grounds on foot.'

'I wonder why they carried out the robbery in Swinford and not in Westport?' put in Teddy. 'Could that mean that someone round here is involved?'

'Yes, and *that* could mean that the cross is still here!'

said Maureen triumphantly. 'They are bound to lie low for a few days!'

'Isn't it exciting!' said Kevin. 'How much is the cross worth?'

'If you just count the value of the gold and the jewelled inlay,' said Con, 'several thousand pounds. However, there is the historical value as well and of course you can't put a price on that. To a private collector, who isn't too particular where he gets things, it would be worth a great deal.'

'Wouldn't it be great if we could find it?' said Teddy. 'Is there a reward?'

'Probably,' said his father. 'But it's hardly likely that it's still in the area. Probably halfway to America or somewhere like that. Lots of rich collectors and no questions asked!'

'Americans aren't all like that,' argued Kevin. 'Uncle Martin lives in America and he's not rich *or* unscrupulous!'

Con McDonagh laughed. 'Always sticking up for somebody, aren't you, Kevin? I didn't mean it that way. I just meant that in a big country there would be a better chance of finding a buyer. Pass the sugar please, someone. My tea's going cold while we're talking about nothing!'

Maureen passed the sugar, wondering how her father could drink tea so calmly when something so exciting had happened — and practically on their own doorstep!

Later that evening, the children left the house to get on with their chores. Maureen had to bring the cow in for milking so the two boys walked up the field with her. Carrots, not wanting to be left out, followed closely.

21

'Wouldn't it be great if we could catch the thieves!' said Teddy. 'Just think ... our names would be in the papers; we'd be famous. And if there was a big reward I'd buy myself a new set of tools and a power-drill like Dad's.'

'I would buy a typewriter,' said Kevin, 'and write letters to all my friends.'

'What would you get, Maureen?' asked Teddy.

'A pony,' answered Maureen promptly. 'One like Liam was riding. I'd groom her and enter her in the county fairs and sell her foals for lots and lots of money.'

Teddy brought them down to earth. 'We've got to find the cross first,' he pointed out. 'And we don't even know if there *is* a reward.'

'Must be,' said Kevin. 'They always give rewards for finding things like that.'

'Come on, Bossy,' called Maureen then, and the little blue cow at the top of the field looked up, then began to trot down the field towards her.

'She's ready for milking,' said Maureen. 'Look, she can't wait to get inside.'

Bossy slowed down as she reached the children, then snorted and continued on down the field to the stone shed where Maureen always milked her. She completely ignored Carrots, who was trotting along beside her. By the time the children had got back down the field she was already in her stall, her ears pricking up as she heard the soft bleating sound from behind the partition in the corner.

'Easy, old girl,' murmured Maureen as she scooped up the tie from between the cow's front legs and then fastened it securely. 'There, you can't walk away from me now. Still know that sound, do you?'

Bossy turned her head slightly, then gave another soft snort. From the corner there came an answering bleat, more like the cry of a lamb than that of a young calf, and Kevin went over to see him.

'When are we putting this calf out, Maureen?' he asked. 'You could put that nose thing on him and let him run with his mother.'

'Dad says there's time enough,' answered Maureen. 'Give me that cloth here, will you? It's a bit cold at night yet and he has all the summer to go outside.'

Kevin put his hand into the enclosure and was met by an eager tongue, then suddenly his hand was drawn right into the young animal's mouth as it commenced to suck at him.

'Hey, let go of my hand, Tiddler!' he objected. 'Your milk isn't ready yet.'

'Shouldn't put your hand in then,' laughed Teddy. 'You know what little calves are like. They will suck anything! I caught that one sucking the dog's tail yesterday. Poor old Carrots was stuck half in and half out of those boards Dad put up for Tiddler, and the silly calf thought the dog was his dinner! He was in a fine state when I rescued him. That daft dog won't go visiting again in a hurry!'

Maureen pulled up the milking stool and very soon the milk was frothing and steaming into the bucket.

'Here it comes,' said Kevin, pulling his hand away at last with great difficulty. 'If you'd just let me go for a minute, I'll get your bucket for you.'

'Thanks,' said Maureen. 'Can you manage to feed him yourself? There's enough milk here now but I can't

23

slow down until Bossy stops letting it down.'

'I'll help him,' said Teddy, taking the half-full bucket and replacing it with a clean one so quickly that Maureen did not have to alter her rhythm at all. 'I'll hold Tiddler back in case he tries to eat Kevin again!'

'Who's eating who?' said Kevin. 'I can look after myself,' making a run at Teddy.

'Will you two stop thumping each other?' said Maureen. 'Bossy may be a quiet cow but she's not going to let me have any milk while you two are having a boxing match behind her. Give her that milk, Kevin ... and don't let the calf drink from that milking bucket. Tip it into the little plastic one for him.'

'When we've finished here,' said Teddy, 'you two come and help me get the hens in, then we'll go up in the tree-house for a while. I want to discuss a few ideas for catching the thieves and getting the reward ... Come on, Kevin, get the milk and hand it in here to me.'

And Teddy leapt nimbly over the partition into the calf's little corner. 'Come on, Tiddler, don't knock me over — here comes your dinner! Milk with milk and milk, and guess what's for pudding? You got it! Milk!'

Later they met in the tree-house, but the discussion achieved very little. Inevitably the conversation drifted again and again to the subject of the reward and what they would do with it. As for a plan of campaign to recover the cross; 'Mayo,' as Teddy pointed out, 'is a very large county. Where do we start?'

And on that rather gloomy note they descended and went to bed.

3 A Mysterious Stranger

As the children were finishing their breakfast next morning, Eileen handed Maureen a parcel.

'What's this?' she asked. 'Present for me?'

'Don't be silly. It's bread. I baked some early this morning, while you three were still asleep, and I thought old Dan might eat some. He likes home-made bread best of all, but he won't be making it himself for a while now. Dad wants you to go over anyway, to arrange about the ass and cart next week. If the weather stays fine we'll be able to bring out that clamp we made last year, and some of the new turf might be ready for moving now.'

'More hard work!' groaned Kevin in mock horror.

'For all the good you are,' said Teddy, 'we might as well leave you at home.'

'Kevin does his best so don't you be teasing him,' said his mother. 'You'll go over to old Dan as soon as you've finished milking, will you, Maureen? And don't take Carrots. You know what he's like when he gets to Dan's fields. He imagines rabbits everywhere. You'd never get home again!'

'I'll put him in the shed so he can't follow us.'

'Good idea. Are you all going then? Don't be too long. Your father wants to go to Castlebar this afternoon and I promised to have the dinner early.'

'Yes, we'll all go,' said Teddy. 'I can't wait to see if the pony has thrown Liam again!'

'Who's Liam?' asked his mother.

'He's a traveller,' said Kevin. 'His family has gone off for the summer and he's got the job of looking after Dan's animals.'

'Just as well,' said Eileen. 'Poor old Dan will be out of action for a while, I expect. An old fellow like that mends slowly. If he has a young buck there to see to the place he will be able to take his time.'

She began clearing the table and the children all went off to do their jobs; Maureen to milk Bossy again, while Teddy looked after his hens and Kevin brought in some vegetables for dinner. Half an hour later the children had all finished and were on their way, the bread safely in Maureen's bicycle basket. As they passed the workshop by the front gate they waved to their father, already busy with an electric saw.

'He didn't hear us,' said Teddy. 'That thing makes an awful racket. When I get one I'm going to fit a silencer to it!'

'I don't suppose Dad likes the noise too much himself,' said Kevin, 'but he couldn't do a job quickly without it. He is making doors for that new house on the main road, and there are hundreds of bits to cut up.'

Dan Moore's house was not very far away. They had to ride down to the main road, cross it, then continue down for half a mile along a dirt track. At this time of year the ruts hardened into odd peaks and ridges, and riding was hard work. Teddy persisted, bouncing his front wheel precariously in and out of the hollows, but Kevin and Maureen preferred to walk and wheel their bicycles. Soon the thin wisp of smoke rising above the thatch was in view, and then they could see the apple

trees which formed a little orchard in front of the house.
Dan Moore's cottage was one of the few thatched
cottages still left in this part of Mayo, and the children
always thought it a lovely sight when they came round
the bend, overgrown at this time of year with straggling
brambles and nettles, and caught their first glimpse of
the faded yellow straw above the apple trees.

'The fire's lit,' said Teddy. 'Liam must be cooking
dinner already!'

'Could be,' said Maureen. 'Let's take the bread in and
see how he is.' She parked her bike at the front gate and
took the bread out carefully. It was still slightly warm
and smelled delicious. 'It's making me hungry,' she
said. 'I'll be ready for some myself when we get back
home.'

'Greedy pig, you've just had breakfast,' said Teddy.

'Have a sniff yourself,' offered Maureen, 'Who's
hungry now!'

They went up the flagged path and Maureen was
about to knock when a voice called, 'Come in.'

She swung the door open and there lay Dan on the
settle bed near the fire, a rug over his legs.

'You're welcome,' he said. 'You'll sit down a while?'

'Mum sent some bread,' said Maureen, drawing up a
chair and sitting down opposite the old man. 'She made
extra because she knew you wouldn't be able to do any
cooking.'

'That's right,' agreed Dan. 'I've a young fellow here
— I believe ye met him yesterday — and he's doing the
bit of cooking for himself and me but I wouldn't be
troubling him for bread. He's enough on his plate, so the
shop bread will do until I'm on my feet again. You'll

thank your mother for me, though, will you?'

'Of course,' said Maureen. 'It's no trouble really, she was baking anyway. Shall I bring you a loaf next time then?'

'Aye,' said Dan. 'I wouldn't say no to that! Anyway, I'll be sending the young lad over to ye for eggs in a day or so. Shop eggs is one thing I'm not keen on if I can get a decent farm egg. Better flavour!'

'The hens are laying well,' said Teddy. 'I'll keep some for you.'

'Good man yourself.' The old man turned his head towards Kevin. 'And how are you, young fellow? Got you working hard for your holidays, have they?'

'Too hard!' agreed Kevin. 'It'll be a holiday when we're back at school!'

'We are starting the turf tomorrow,' said Maureen. 'That's the other reason why we've come. Dad will be needing the ass and cart some time next week if the weather stays good — and if it's all right with you, of course.'

'And why wouldn't it? You can just see me sitting in a cart right now, can't you?' Old Dan chuckled. 'The doctor says I'll be off my feet for a few weeks yet, so you're welcome to it of course. Why don't you put the kettle on the gas cooker here, Maureen, and make us a cup of tea while you're here? Young Liam is out in the barns and I don't want to keep calling him in for everything — it's a busy time of year and some of the jobs are new to him.'

'How is he managing?' asked Teddy.

'Oh, he's great. He's a willing youngster, strong too, and he can manage those ponies. Not many young

28

fellows I'd trust with the bloodstock, but he's worked odd times for me before so I knew he was up to it. Bit of luck getting him really — he's getting his keep and the bit of pocket-money from me, but he's certainly earning it. I think the arrangement is suiting the pair of us nicely.'

'Shall I call him in for a cup of tea?' asked Kevin.

Dan shook his head. 'You could take one out to him when we've had ours. But he'll be too busy to come in. He's a young calf there that's been sick with the scour and he's had to take it off the mother and bucket feed it with glucose, and then there's the cow to milk after that and she's not taking too well to it.'

'It's a bit late in the year for calving anyway,' said Maureen. 'Our cow calved late, too, and we were ages without milk.'

'This isn't the house cow,' said Dan, 'she's a suckler. He'll be putting the calf back on her as soon as it is clear. It's just that it's an extra job right now when we don't want one. Still, I must say the lad is coping.'

'Kettle's boiling,' said Kevin. 'Give me the teapot and I'll make it.'

'You could get a slice of that bread,' said Dan, 'and ye might all eat a piece as well.'

Teddy looked hopefully at Maureen but she cut just two slices and wrapped the rest up again.

'We have some at home,' she said, trying not to look too hungrily at the fragrant slices. 'This is for you. Anyway, we had breakfast not long ago.'

'And now,' said Dan, 'what's this business about a stolen cross at the community centre? I heard the end of the news on the radio but I missed half the details.'

29

As Kevin poured the tea and handed it round, Teddy told Dan the story of the kidnapping and the stolen cross. Dan looked suitably impressed and Teddy was about to add a few embellishments of his own but Kevin was worried about Liam.

'Do you think we should take his tea out to him before it gets cold?' he asked.

'You shouldn't have poured it out till we'd finished,' said Maureen. 'Anyway, I suppose we'd better go on out with it. And we should be going ourselves.'

'Mum is having dinner early,' said Kevin. 'Dad is off to Castlebar. He might take us if we're quick.'

'Off with you then. You can fill my cup again before you go and tell Liam not to hurry back in.'

The barns at the back of Dan's house were across a paved yard. They skirted several bales of barbed wire, obviously intended by Dan for some fencing before his accident, which had been left right in the path of anyone walking round the corner by the water-butt.

'That's dangerous,' said Teddy. 'Do you think we should move them over beside the sheds?'

'Liam might not like it if we start interfering,' said Kevin. 'He's supposed to be in charge while old Dan is laid up.'

'I don't think he would mind a bit of help,' said Maureen. 'He probably has a lot of more important jobs to do. You two put them over there where it's safer, and I'll go and find Liam with this tea and slice of bread.'

'Just like old Bossyboots, leaving us the hard work!' said Teddy. 'Oh, well — I suppose I asked for it, opening my big mouth! Come on then, Kevin. Do you see that wire loop sticking up? You get hold of that and

30

I'll take this end. Careful now, if it touches your leg it will scratch you.'

'I ought to know how to handle this stuff by now,' retorted Kevin. 'I'm not a baby, you know.'

'Okay, then. One—two—three—lift!' Teddy's side lifted by several inches but Kevin's did not budge.

'It's no good!' gasped Kevin. 'I can't lift the loop without touching the barbs. We'll have to roll it. I suppose that's why Liam didn't move it — he couldn't lift it on his own!'

'I'll get two shovels so,' said Teddy. 'We'll lever it up and roll it over to the corner of the yard.'

He looked around and caught sight of an old crowbar. 'Just the job! You take that shovel over there, and I'll lever with the crowbar. Each time I lift it, you give it a roll in that direction.' Suiting his actions to his words, Teddy wedged the crowbar under the nearest bale and pushed down hard. The wire moved forward several inches, and then, as Kevin pushed the top loops with the edge of his spade, the entire bale moved forward several feet.

'Great job! We'll be done in a few minutes.'

While the boys were wrestling with the barbed wire, Maureen had gone round the other side of the barns. These were a succession of sheds, joined together by virtue of having been built one against the other so that they all leaned rather drunkenly towards the most ancient, with its rusted galvanised iron roof tied down with equally rusty wire. Several of the barns had no doors, but those which did were closed and bolted. The last shed, however, had two half doors of which the upper was open and the lower closed. Maureen guessed that this must be the barn housing the sick calf, and the most likely place to look for Liam. Sure enough, as she reached the door and looked in over the top, she could make out in the semi-darkness the outline of a young animal lying in a stall. Two crudely tied planks kept him in his corner, and knowing that he could not escape even if she opened the lower door, Maureen let herself in and slipped the catch shut again by leaning over the frame.

There was no sign of Liam so she put the tea on a flag shelf high in the wall and carefully balanced the bread on top of the cup. Then she approached the calf, talking softly to him so that he would not be afraid of her. He was watching her now, and gave a little mooing sound as she came nearer. Then he scrambled to his feet and gave one long and rather wobbly stretch. Maureen laughed at him.

'There's not much wrong with you if you can stretch like that! You'll be back to your mother soon, I'd say.'

The calf nuzzled up to her and she began to scratch it behind one ear. Then, concluding that no food was on the menu just then, he relaxed back on to his bedding again. Checking first to see that the straw was fairly clean, Maureen sat down beside him to wait for Liam. She had only been there for a moment when she heard voices, and decided that Liam must have found her brothers and was coming with them to find her. She was about to go out when she suddenly realised that the voices did not belong to Teddy and Kevin at all! Then she heard somebody say, 'Are you sure you weren't followed?' That was Liam's voice, she was sure.

Then a strange voice, lower and rather slurred,

answered, 'Quite sure. If you'll just hide me for a few days till they stop looking for that cross, I'll be fine. Right now there are too many guards about for safety. If they stop me and start asking questions, I'll be for it. We'd do well to wait till this business is over. They'll have forgotten all about it in a week or so, and then I can walk up to Dan's door and introduce myself as though I've just arrived in the Swinford area. He might know of some other local farmer needing a lad, and I could go odd-jobbing like you. No questions asked!'

'That's all very well for you, Pat,' said Liam, 'but what about me? I've a job here, and I like Dan ... I'd stay on permanently if he wants me. If the police find me helping you I could be in trouble too. And another thing ... who says they don't know you? You were here a couple of years back when you all spent a few weeks up at Foxford, and you haven't changed that much.'

'Right! But there's no need for them to see me, is there? And as for you, we could say you didn't know anything if they did happen to catch up with me. After all, you didn't steal anything. It's myself that's the thief!'

'Don't talk like that,' said Liam. 'It's over now. Best to put it behind you. Now you come with me and I'll show you where you can stay. There's new hay in the hayshed, just brought in, and I've put a couple of old blankets up there for you. You can stay there and around these sheds. Dan will be stuck in the house for a few weeks yet so he won't see you. If anyone comes round you'd best stay hidden though. Dan doesn't get many visitors, but you never know!'

In her stall, Maureen was frozen with fear. 'Pat' must

be the thief who had stolen the cross from the museum curator — and Liam was going to hide him! What did that make him? She tried to think of the phrase her father had used about someone who had stood by while a robbery was committed, 'an accessory after the fact'. How dreadful! And if they knew she had overheard them they might — Maureen tried not to imagine what might happen. She closed her eyes and tried not to think about it at all. Perhaps they would go away in a moment, and then she could creep out and pretend she hadn't heard anything.

But Pat and Liam seemed rooted to the spot. There was a brief silence and then she heard the strange voice saying, 'Cigarette?'

'No, ' said Liam. 'Don't use them. Anyway, I've got to be getting back to work. There's a load of wire in the yard back there to be shifted. I didn't get a chance to move it yet — too heavy. You can give me a hand with it while you're here ... That is, if we haven't got visitors. I thought I heard voices just now. I'll go round the barn and see. You'd better go into the shed here until I call you.'

Hardly daring to breathe, Maureen crouched further back into the corner, moving stealthily so as not to excite the calf, as Pat slipped the catch and opened the lower half door. Luckily he didn't seem interested in the calf and that corner was gloomy enough anyway. He stood in the doorway with his back to her, cigarette in hand, eyes fixed on the scene before him. Maureen could only hope nothing would panic him into coming further into the shed. Where were those boys?

Then she heard Liam greeting them. Pat tensed,

dropping his half-finished cigarette on to the floor and putting his foot on it. But he didn't move from where he was standing.

After what seemed like an interminable pause, she heard Liam's voice saying 'Good-bye' to the boys, speaking loudly as if to warn Pat to stay hidden. Another minute, thought Maureen, and they'll be gone and Pat will go and I can get out. But just then she heard Kevin calling, 'Where's Maureen? We'd better wait for her.'

'Maureen? Was she with you?' asked Liam.

Stupid, stupid Kevin, Maureen silently raged. Now they'd all come looking for her. Luckily Teddy broke in, 'She's gone back to talk to Dan. Come on, if we don't hurry we'll miss the ride to Castlebar.'

'Don't mind about me,' thought Maureen in wry amusement, thanking her lucky stars for Teddy's fib.

Liam came back, whistling to himself. 'Come on, Pat,' he called. 'It was just two of the neighbours. I'll show you that hay before I get back to work. They did the wire for me, so I can get straight on with something else.'

Maureen's relief was indescribable as she finally tumbled out of her cramped hiding-place. She ran around the house and straight into old Dan's kitchen, gasping for breath as she came in.

'What on earth is the matter?' asked Dan. 'Seen a leprechaun?'

Maureen laughed, trying to gloss over her excitement. 'Not at all! I've been searching for Liam to give him the tea but I couldn't find him. I left the tea in one of the barns.'

'Oh, good enough,' said Dan. 'He maybe went up the back fields. I'll see him when he comes in and he can have a fresh cup. Do you want another one yourself?'

'Oh no! I mean, thanks, but I must be off. The boys have gone already and I'll have to catch them up.'

'Goodbye so,' said Dan. 'I'll send himself up in a day or two for eggs ...' but she was already out of the cottage. She could hardly wait to tell the boys what she overheard.

4 What Maureen Overheard

Maureen pedalled back down the narrow lane at break-neck speed, this time disregarding the pot-holes which threatened to bounce her into the nearest ditch at any moment. Bucking the wheels in and out of the ruts, and narrowly missing an extra large subsidence, she reached the main road in time to see Teddy's colourful 'killer' pennant fluttering above his back wheel just before it disappeared round a bend. She forced herself to wait while a car went past, then raced across the highway and into the lane which led up to Rinn Mór.

'Hi! Teddy!' she yelled, forcing her legs to turn the wheels faster up the gentle slope. 'Teddy, stop!'

The pennant went on bobbing up and down obstinately. Teddy could not hear her!

'Kevin! Teddy! Wait for me!'

The lane was becoming gradually steeper and she needed all her breath to stay in control of the bicycle. Then to her relief as she rounded the next bend she saw that Kevin's bike had slipped its chain and the boys had stopped to fix it.

'Didn't you hear me calling you?' she puffed, lifting her feet thankfully. No brakes were needed — the bicycle stopped obligingly on its own.

'What's wrong?' asked Teddy. 'We didn't want to wait for you, nattering to old Dan. If we're quick we might get a ride to Castlebar with Dad after dinner.'

'Everything's wrong! I've got to talk to you now!'

'All right,' said Teddy, 'but it had better be good!'

Maureen dropped her bike on to the grass verge and took a deep breath.

'I've just overheard a very interesting conversation. I reckon Liam is mixed up in the cross affair.'

'I don't believe you,' said Kevin immediately. 'He wouldn't do a thing like that.'

'I don't think he would either,' said Teddy. 'What makes you so sure?'

'Well,' began Maureen dramatically, 'you just listen to what *I* heard just now!' And she began, with great satisfaction, to relate the conversation she had overheard in the shed at Dan Moore's. 'There,' she concluded triumphantly when she had given them all the details she could remember. 'Doesn't that sound funny to you?'

'Are you sure that's what they were saying?' said Kevin. 'All that about hiding from guards and everything? Couldn't you have made a mistake?'

'I don't see how,' said Maureen. 'They were talking

38

about trouble with the police and stealing things, and I was only a few feet away. Doesn't it all fit in? After all, we know the cross went missing not far from here. Isn't it possible — even likely — that local people may have been involved? And you never know, the cross may be hidden right now on Dan Moore's land!'

'Well, I'm going to ask Liam straight out,' said Teddy. 'I'm not afraid of him or any thieves, and I'm not sure whether I believe he's guilty or not. There's only one way to find out!'

'I don't believe it,' announced Kevin, 'and I think you two are horrible. I like Liam and I don't believe he would kidnap those men or tie them up. You've made a mistake. They were probably talking about something quite different, and ,anyway, you shouldn't have been listening!'

With that, Kevin righted his bike, tested the pedal with one foot to make sure the chain was back in place properly, and cycled off up the hill on his own.

'Let him go,' said Maureen. 'He'll calm down in a little while. You know what he's like when he gets annoyed. Especially when he is sticking up for someone.'

'I don't know why he should be so upset about Liam,' said Teddy. 'After all, we've only just met him and we don't really know anything about him.'

'I know what I heard,' answered Maureen. 'I think Liam and this fellow Pat are criminals.'

'Well, I'm going to find out for sure. Come on, let's get back home. I'm hungry and I want an outing with Dad, Liam or no Liam. Might get a rest from all the hard work!'

For the rest of that day Kevin avoided them, disappearing straight after dinner when his father announced that he was leaving for Castlebar, and watching sulkily from the safety of the tree-house as Maureen and Teddy piled into the back seat of the old Ford. Let them go! he grumbled to himself. He was going to spend his afternoon in comfort, reading the comics he had bought last week in town and had not yet had time to read. Sometimes he wished he was the only child in the family. How peaceful everything would be then!

Not until he heard the car turning into the gateway, some three hours later, did he rearrange his comics into a neat pile and prepare to come down from his hide-out. His eyes were smarting from the small print and his limbs were stiff from sitting so long in one position so he decided to take refuge from any further discussion about Liam or the cross by being somebody else for the remainder of the day. When Teddy bounced up to the tree waving an open bag of crisps in one hand and a half-eaten orange in the other, Kevin was ready.

'Mission control to Houston! Stand by for splash-down!' and he landed in a stiff heap at Teddy's feet.

'What do you think you're doing?' demanded Teddy. 'There are crisps in the car if you're interested.'

'Over and out!' continued Kevin in a monotonous falsetto, rising to his feet and stretching his arms out in front of him. 'We require protein pills and fresh water. Our masters from the planet Mars greet you Earthling!'

'We have ways of making you talk!' mocked Teddy, and turned away in disgust. 'You're potty!'

'I am a Robot Mark 59!' announced Kevin and

marched stiffly towards the car. 'Take me to your leader!'

'Dad's in the kitchen having a cup of tea,' called Teddy over his shoulder. 'You can come in for some if it won't rust your insides!'

He departed and Kevin, just in case anyone was still looking, continued to the car as a robot, reached through the window and retrieved his crisps, then proceeded stiff-legged to the kitchen.

'We require supplies!' he announced.

'He's in one of his silly moods,' said Maureen. 'Don't take any notice.'

'Milk or an oilcan?' asked Teddy politely.

'I am programmed for milk and sugar,' replied the robot. He seated himself one limb at a time and continued to gaze wide-eyed out of the window.

'Too much TV,' commented his father. 'He'd better have an early night. You three are booked to turn some of that turf tomorrow!'

'Oh, no!' said Teddy. 'I had other plans.'

'They'll have to wait till the evening,' said Eileen. 'You've had nearly a whole day free today. You know your father promised you extra pocket-money for these summer jobs. You can't expect to earn it doing nothing!'

'Did you hear the news while we were out?' asked Con.

'I did. It's promised fine the next couple of days so that hay might be ready to come in by Friday.... There was some more about the stolen cross, too.'

'Oh, what?' asked Maureen eagerly. 'They haven't found it, have they?'

'No, not exactly. But apparently someone saw the

thieves leaving the community centre and they were heading south.'

'How did they know they were the thieves?' asked Kevin, suddenly forgetting he was meant to be a robot.

'The man who saw them said one of them was carrying a blue briefcase, and they were coming from the direction of the grounds. I told you before, the cross was packed in a blue briefcase!'

'And we are south of the community centre!' shouted Teddy. 'They may have even come by this road!'

'It could be still around here somewhere!' added Maureen. 'They may have hidden it somewhere until they could get back to collect it.'

'Or until the guards stop searching,' said Teddy. 'I'm going on a cross hunt tonight!'

That evening, Teddy and Maureen finished their jobs at top speed and departed up the road to look for the briefcase. It was a frustrating job however, and they soon realised it.

'We don't even know how big it is,' complained Maureen in disgust. 'It could be just anywhere.'

'If I was hiding a briefcase,' said Teddy, 'I'd put it in one of the old ruins. There are loads of tumble-down barns.'

'That's just it. We could never search all of them.'

'I think we should give up for tonight. What we need is a Clue!'

When they returned home Kevin was already in bed, and at their mother's insistance the two older ones decided to go off as well. They would have to be up early next day, after all, and the sooner they set out the sooner they would be back home to resume the search!

5 Turning the Turf

Next morning they were all up at seven. While they were seeing to the cow and calf, their mother packed a flask of tea, bottles of orange squash and water, packets of sandwiches and apples, and several bags of crisps in two duffle bags. She knew from experience that in spite of a good breakfast, turning turf was a sure way of bringing on hunger pangs. Maureen and Teddy were to take a bag each while Kevin was entrusted with a bag of sweets which would fit comfortably into his pocket. He appeared to be more friendly this morning so Teddy and Maureen continued to avoid the subject of the cross.

The road to the bog was long enough if one had to walk all the way, but to the three children with their bicycles the distance seemed just right. It was a lovely day after some drizzle overnight and the weather was just right for cycling, warm and still but not too hot, and they were glad that they had decided to wear shorts instead of the jeans their mother had left out for them. It was nearly three miles into Swinford town and their route lay through the main street and under the old railway bridge to the back road which led to the bog. Normally at this time of day the street would have been deserted but today it was full of stall-holders setting up their trestles for business and spreading out their wares for people to inspect.

'Forgot it was market day today,' said Maureen. 'We should have brought some pocket-money with us. I need some new markers for school.'

'There's another fair before we go back,' said Teddy. 'Just as well we're out early! We'd never ride through this lot once the crowd gets here.'

The boys were inclined to linger before the various stalls but before long there was a warning shout.

'Come on, you two!' called Maureen from the far end of the street. 'We'll be all day getting there if you don't hurry up.'

'Coming!' shouted Teddy. 'Bet you I'll be there before you!'

Maureen began pedalling furiously and as the boys rounded the corner under the bridge she was already out of sight. She kept well ahead of them for the next two miles but then they managed to catch her at the fork where they were to branch off for the bog.

'That's not fair!' gasped Maureen as they drew level with her. 'I couldn't cross the main road because there were cattle turning down towards Killasser and I had to stop for them. I should be given a head-start when things like that happen!'

Twenty minutes later they were on the rough track leading down through the turf banks to their own plot. The surface was uneven and stony, and even Teddy had to slow down to a crawl. Tractors, carts, and the huge turf-cutting machine had all contributed to the deep ruts and pot-holes, and patches of mud and broken turf added to the difficulty of keeping cycle wheels straight. The children had sometimes seen cars on these tracks, and even the best drivers had been forced to creep along in first gear. They were all pleased to reach the lone willow which marked their bank.

'We'll have tea before we start,' said Maureen, 'and then we can work for a couple of hours straight.'

'Why don't we have our sandwiches now?' said Teddy. 'Then we wouldn't have to find a place to leave them!'

'No way!' said Maureen. 'Then you'd be wanting to go home at two o'clock! A cup of tea is all you get now.' She took the duffle bag off her shoulders and let it slide to the ground. 'I think the drinks are in yours, Teddy. This is the one with the food in it.'

Teddy slung his bag to the ground. 'Crash! Yes, that must be the drinks department!'

'If you've broken Mum's thermos you'll be for it,' said Maureen. 'Give it to me.'

'There are only two cups,' pointed out Kevin. 'Someone will have to drink from the thermos.'

'I brought a plastic beaker,' said Maureen scornfully. 'If it was up to you two, nothing would be remembered. Now sit down, shut up, and if you're lucky you'll get a drink!'

As they drank the hot tea, which always seemed to taste so much better in the open air, their eyes took in the familiar scene before them, the ridges of bog stretching away to the pale blue mountains on the horizon, the sparkle of the lake away to their right, the silver heads of the bog cotton dancing in the wind, the bright gold of the gorse and the vivid crimson splash of rhododendron around the small cottages in the glen. And in the silence, borne on the soft sweet wind, all the sounds of the bog came to them clearly. The unseen cascade of the skylarks, the gurgling of a hidden mountain stream, the plaintive calling of sheep, the lonely cry of a lapwing.

45

After they had finished their tea, they reluctantly hung their duffle bags on their bike handlebars and propped the bikes against a ragged swamp willow, out of the reach of questing dogs.

'Look,' whispered Kevin, 'there's Mr. Durkan.'

In the next cutting to theirs, a sturdy figure was already hard at work.

'Let's go over to watch him,' said Teddy.

'We'd better get started,' Maureen objected.

'Ah, but he's a real expert, part of our national heritage,' said Teddy persuasively. 'Do you realise that in a few years' time there won't be any Mr. Durkans left?'

'Just for a few minutes,' urged Kevin.

'All right,' agreed Maureen reluctantly, knowing well their interest was not so much in watching a master at work as in getting a few minutes' respite.

They crossed over their own cutting, down nearly six feet into the swampy ground which separated the two banks, then across the treacherous lumps of caved-in turf and heather left after years of turf cutting by the machine.

'I see you're cutting by hand,' called Maureen when they reached him.

'Aye. Eighty yards the machine did but he couldn't get into the far corner without shooting it all into the swamp, so I'm doing a few yards myself by slane.'

'Can we watch?' asked Kevin. 'I'd love to see how they used to do it. Mum and Dad are always talking about it.'

'You can, of course,' chuckled Mr. Durkan. 'You can even try the slane yourself, if you like!'

'Great!' shouted Kevin.

'That big yoke does a great job on the turf,' said Mr. Durkan, 'but it ruins the bog. Look at all that good turf, all wasted. Those treads go too near the edge and the lot caves in, down here into the hole. When it was all cut by hand there was nothing wasted. Enough turf for hundreds of years here if it's respected.'

'What will they do with the bog when all the turf is cut?' asked Kevin.

'Maybe start again on the next layer,' said Mr. Durkan. 'And maybe just bulldoze it flat, put a drain or two in, and plant trees on it again for the forestry. It was all forest once, you know.'

'Yes, the turf is just dead trees and things,' said Teddy. 'We did that at school.'

'They use turf to grow seeds,' said Maureen. 'Dad says it's pure fertiliser.'

'That's right,' agreed Mr. Durkan. 'Don't fall in there, young fellow ... some of those pools are deep. Follow me now. This is where we climb up.'

The bank came down to meet the water here and it was an easy job to climb up on to the side. Beyond, the rows of machine-cut sods lay drying in the sun, but here the squat sodden bricks of slane turf were piled in heaps.

'I cut so many,' explained Mr. Durkan, 'then I barrow them out and spread them to dry. You can see why the machine couldn't get this bit,' and he pointed to the slope. 'If he went too close he'd send that lot into the water and it would be no good at all, and if he cut further back the boom would send the turf into the water altogether on the other side. That would work in a really good summer, but the way things usually are I'd be until the next year drying it !'

47

'Why is the bank so narrow here?' asked Teddy.

'That's obvious!' said Maureen. 'In the old days they never dreamt of machine cutting so there was no need to leave a wide piece. They cut both sides of the bank at once, as near as possible to the road so they could get it out easily.'

'Quite right,' said Mr. Durkan. 'It was all slanes and donkeys then. Sometimes we'd camp out here for a few days to save the time going back and forward to the house.'

'Must have been fun,' said Kevin.

'Not for me,' shuddered Maureen. 'Too many midges when the sun goes in! What did you do when it rained?'

'Got wet!' laughed the old man. 'Come on, let's see some of you cut a sod.'

Teddy was the first taker for the slane which he held out. It was rather like a spade, with a ridge on top for his foot and another ridge down one side.

'Different counties had different slanes,' explained Mr. Durkan. 'This here is a Mayoman's slane. The best sort!'

Teddy balanced the slane on the bank, then pushed downwards. A large clod parted from the edge and dropped into the water.

'Great stuff!' Maureen couldn't resist saying. 'Look out, everyone ... expert at work!'

'Sideways,' advised Mr. Durkan. 'Look, at right angles to the face.' He took the slane and demonstrated. A perfect sod of turf went flying over to join the pile on the bank.

'Let me try again,' said Teddy. He managed a rather mis-shapen sod which sailed over the pile and on to the heather beyond, but his third attempt produced a perfect block and he proudly flicked it on to the heap.

'There! Did it!'

'Good!' acknowledged Mr. Durkan. 'Does anyone else want to try?'

'Yes, please,' said Kevin eagerly, but he was too small to handle the long tool and relinquished it to Maureen, disappointment on his face. She managed to produce a passable sod on her second attempt, and lifted it carefully on to the bank.

'Now you're all old hands,' announced Mr. Durkan. 'And you'd better get back to your own work and let me get on with mine!'

'How much do you think we'll get done today,' asked Teddy as they walked back. 'I'm hoping to buy that alarm clock I saw in Mum's catalogue, and I only need two more pounds.'

'It's a pity Dad offered to pay us for doing this job!' said Maureen. 'Now all you'll be talking about is how much money you'll be earning. Between holiday job money and rewards for finding stolen crosses, you might do better to go and live in a bank!'

'Well, I think it's only right that we get paid,' said Teddy. 'After all, we're working hard here and I think we've earned a bit extra. If we had to buy turf by the trailer you know how much that would cost.'

'All the same, it's just another farm job,' said Maureen. 'Kids didn't get paid for jobs like this in the old days, and they worked far harder than we do now. Dad and Mum both had to do this in their time, and they had to cut it with a slane as well.'

'The old days were different,' piped up Kevin. 'And I

guess I agree with Teddy, I wouldn't enjoy it so much if I didn't have a chance to earn some wages too!'

'We'll aim at thirty yards today then,' said Maureen. 'I think if we do that much we'll have done well. We'll go as far as that bend where the machine overshot the bank, and then we'll stop for some food! Now come on ... and no more talking.'

They separated and began the slow, back-breaking job of turning the sods, a job they had to do every year after the turf-cutting machine had spread the sods out on the top of the turf bank. If the weather held they were able to turn the turves quite soon, but if the spring was damp, as this one had been, they had to wait until the wind and sun had dried out the upper crust so that the turf would not crumble when they turned it. Their father used a fork for turning but the children preferred the easy rhythm of bending from the waist, then reaching forwards. The surfaces were uncomfortable to handle as they had dried out unevenly, leaving little spikes and snags sticking up here and there to tear the skin. The trick, as they had worked out for themselves, was not to grasp the sods too tightly but to allow their hands to glide over them, pulling them easily forward.

They worked in silence for what seemed an age. Kevin was the first to pause and stand upright.

'Who's that?' he asked suddenly, pointing to the tractor and trailer which had drawn up on the dirt road.

'That's Ger McDonagh,' said Maureen. 'He's some relation of Dad's, I think. He brings cattle and stuff for people with his tractor.'

'I mean the other one on the trailer,' said Kevin.

They all looked where he was pointing. Above the

50

crossbar of the trailer a mop of red curls could just be seen.

'It's Liam!' said Teddy. 'He must be taking some turf home for Dan.'

Sure enough, the driver had leapt down and was asking the boy in the trailer for directions. Then the children saw the red-haired lad swing himself down, nod, then point to the near end of a large clamp.

'It's Liam right enough!' agreed Maureen. 'Never mind him now, he has his job and we have ours.'

The trio turned once more to their work, but Teddy kept glancing over his shoulder and found it difficult to concentrate on what he was doing. When the last sod was loaded on the trailer, Ger swung a sack down to Liam from the tractor seat and started up the motor. A cloud of black smoke was coughed into the air and then the tractor chugged away slowly. Liam sat down on the rough grass and opened the sack.

'He's having his lunch,' said Teddy. 'I'm going over to have a chat with him. You two get our lunch ready and I'll be back in a few minutes!'

Before either of the others could object he was half-way down the bank, jumping over the clumps of heather and avoiding the deeper ruts. Liam saw him coming and waved.

'Hi, Teddy. I saw you over there. Hard work?'

'Hard enough,' shouted Teddy. He raced up to Liam's patch of grass and sank down to his knees, panting. 'Didn't expect to see you here.'

'That's last year's turf,' explained Liam. 'Dan wanted it brought home to make room for the new clamps. There are only two trailers left in it. Ger will be back in an hour, but there was no point in me going back. He has a tipper and he'll dump it by the house. It's a rough ride back with the turf! Once is plenty for me.'

'How is Dan?'

'Great! I left him with the radio on full volume and a big pot of tea. He'll be all right till I get back. Ger said he'd go in the house and see if he needed anything else.'

'Great to be able to trust people,' agreed Teddy. 'Ger *is* trustworthy, isn't he?'

'I expect so,' said Liam, puzzled. 'Why?'

'Well, you know. Can't trust just anybody.'

'What do you mean by that?'

'You should know. Some people steal things, given the chance.'

'Are you hinting at something?'

'Maybe.'

'Oh, you can stop that "maybe" business. Talk plain! Look, are you upset about something? Do you want to talk about it?'

'It could be yourself I'm upset about,' he said finally. 'All right, I'll talk to you straight. I'm not afraid of you, even if you are involved with it. You're only a kid, not much older than me.'

'Involved with what? Look, let's talk. I think you've made a mistake about something, and if you think I had anything to do with it I have a right to know.'

'All right! Now, I've heard that there's been some trouble — stealing and the like — and you were involved. Is that true?'

'Indeed it is not! I stole nothing! Who told you that?'

Teddy stood up. 'It's not important who told me. You

52

were heard talking to a fellow about trouble with the police and stealing. There's been only one theft around here — the Westport cross. Now tell me it wasn't you and some of your pals!'

Liam sprang to his feet in a rage. 'How dare you say that! I tell you, I stole nothing and I don't know anything about that cross. Sure I heard about it — didn't everybody? — but it was nothing to do with me. You're saying that because I'm a traveller, aren't you? Go on, admit it!' With that, Liam drew back his right fist and brought it forward sharply into Teddy's left shoulder. Luckily Liam knew nothing about boxing or Teddy could have been hurt. As it was he went sprawling on to the ground. He rolled over on his back and was about to stand up, but the sight of Liam looming menacingly above him made him decide to stay where he was!

Catching his breath, Liam went straight on, 'Dan Moore trusts me! I've worked odd jobs for him this last couple of years and he knows I'm no thief. He gives me money for the shopping or anything else that's needed and he knows I'd not steal a penny of it. So there, Teddy McDonagh!'

Teddy gulped. 'Honest, I didn't say that because you're a traveller. I said it because ... well, you were heard talking to a fellow about being wanted by the police and hiding him at Moore's ...'

'Oh, it's that you're on about, is it? Well first of all, let me tell you that lad has nothing to do with the Westport cross. And second, he may be staying at Dan's place, but he is not taking anything from Dan. I'm feeding him myself, out of my own wages. And third, it's none of your business!'

'But it is,' insisted Teddy. 'If you're hiding a dangerous criminal ...'

'Dangerous criminal is it now? Well, I'll show you what sort of dangerous criminal he is! I'm busy all day today but you come on over tonight around eight when I've a bit of time to spare and I'll show you exactly who it is I'm hiding. Will that satisfy you?'

'Yes,' said Teddy, scrambling to his feet. 'I guess it will.'

'That is, of course, if you're not afraid of a dangerous criminal. Are you?'

'I'm not,' said Teddy quickly, hoping he wasn't.

'Good enough. And you believe me?'

'I think I do,' said Teddy soberly. 'Yes, I really think I do. I'll be there.'

He returned to Maureen and Kevin a lot more slowly than he had left them.

'Well?' asked Maureen.

Teddy sat down and looked at his feet. 'I think we may have made a mistake,' he said. 'Liam says he didn't have anything to do with it.'

'Didn't I say that?' pointed out Kevin.

'What made you change your mind?' said Maureen.

'I'm not sure. He's going to tell me the whole story tonight. I have to go over and visit him and meet this other fellow.'

'We'll all go,' said Kevin.

'No. Just me. You're not invited.'

'But what if it's a trap? What if they are going to kidnap you?' asked Maureen.

Teddy helped himself to a sandwich. 'That's a chance I'll have to take!'

54

6 Carrots in Trouble

At five that afternoon three tired children arrived back at Rinn Mór. They were very pleased to see the dinner waiting for them, and attacked it as though they had not eaten for a week!

'I told you the bog is great for giving kids an appetite!' laughed Eileen. 'More, Teddy?'

'Please!' echoed three voices in unison.

'It was hard work,' said Kevin, attacking his third helping of cold beef. 'I'm starving'.

Even Teddy, however, finally had to admit that he had really had enough, and reluctantly got to his feet.

'I'm off to feed the hens,' he announced.

Only one wellington, however, was to be seen outside the kitchen door.

'Hey, you lot! Has one of you hidden my boot?' he called. 'Come on, I want to get the hens locked in early so I can get on with something else.'

'I haven't seen it,' said Mrs. McDonagh. 'Did you wear them this morning when you went out to help feed the calf?'

'I did, and I left them outside the door. Now there's only one there.'

'Well, you know where *that's* gone.' said Kevin. 'There's only one fellow round here that would hide one boot and I'll give you a clue! He's got red hair and he is always hungry and he is specially fond of nibbling things ...'

'I might have guessed!' said Teddy in disgust. 'Carrots, of course! Well, you'll have to go and find it, Kevin. I can't go out with one boot on and I'm not putting my runners back on if I have to scratch through all the barns!'

'I'll go,' offered Maureen. 'I've eaten so much today I'll burst if I don't move! Come on, Kevin.'

'He was up the fields when we came home. I saw him running back down the fields to meet us,' said Kevin. 'He probably went back up there with the boot. You know he's always finding new hiding-places for his trophies!'

Maureen laughed. 'Between chewing all the boots he can get his teeth into and nibbling at all the plants in the garden, he must be the most useless dog anyone ever had. Why don't you trade him in for another one?'

'He'll grow out of it,' said Kevin firmly. 'He's my dog and I wouldn't swap him for any other dog in the world!'

They set off for the fort, whistling from time to time. No dog answered!

'Carrots!' called Kevin as they neared the fort. 'Are you there, boy?'

At last an answering yap sounded from the huge blackberry bush on the slope, and Maureen groaned. 'Guess where his new hidey-hole is? Bet it's in there, right in the middle of all those thorns!'

'Woof!' agreed Carrots. They could hear his tail thumping madly up and down on the dry earth around the blackberry roots.

Kevin flattened himself on his stomach and peered down under the bush.

'You little rat! I can see it, Maureen, but it's right in there at the back. We can't possibly reach it unless we cut back some of those branches. I'd better go down to the house and get Dad's sickle.'

'You're too young.,'said Maureen. 'Dad would have a fit if he saw you carrying that thing. You know how he feels about sharp tools. I'll go and get it and you stay here in case that idiot dog comes out with the boot.'

'Okay!' Kevin rolled over on to his back and stared at the sky. It was pleasant up here and he felt that he might go to sleep but for the slight dampness which still clung to the grass. After his hard day at the bog, followed by the huge dinner he had eaten, it would be all too easy to doze off! Clearly the damp had not deterred Carrots. He was quite dry and cosy in his blackberry bush!

'Carrots!' he called softly. 'Carrots! Come on, bring it out here. Aren't you tired too?'

Carrots gave an answering whine and crawled out, wagging his tail and panting.

'You didn't bring the boot? No, I somehow didn't think you would! Wonder what else you've got hidden in there? Come on, then ... lie down and stop licking my face. You'll lick me away..'

Carrots obediently stretched out beside his master, then suddenly sat up again and cocked his head.

'What's wrong, old boy? Think you're hearing rabbits again, do you?'

Carrots gave a low growl and Kevin tensed as he heard men's voices beyond the fort. The wind was blowing lightly in his direction and he could hear the voices more and more plainly as the two men approached. Just as he thought they were going to climb

57

up the other slope and discover him, he heard one man
telling the other to stop. Kevin put one arm around
the dog's neck, hoping that he would stay quiet, and
tried to keep as still as possible. Perhaps it was just two
of the neighbours taking a short cut across the fields, but
somehow that didn't seem right. Carrots knew all the
neighbours and would not growl if he recognised a
voice. No, these had to be strangers! Then again...
Perhaps they were Liam and the other boy Maureen had
overheard!

'The hay has been two days in the cocks already,' one
of the men was saying. 'They'll be bringing it in soon.
They don't leave it too long in this country. If the
weather stays fine now they may even chance it Friday.'

That wasn't Liam anyway. Kevin knew his voice, and
this was a man's voice. 'You and Ned will have to come
back tonight and get it.'

'Why not now?' asked the other man. Kevin was relieved to find that he did not recognise this voice either. Good — perhaps Liam was not involved after all!

'It's safer to leave it where it is. If anyone sees us here in the daylight we're just crossing a field, but if we start moving stones, somebody might put two and two together! There's always somebody watching or listening.'

'Which stone is it under, then?'

'That one over there. It slipped right under when I tried to weight it down. Don't touch it till well after dark. Midnight should be all right, or maybe you should leave it till one to make quite sure there's no one around. Then you can go straight down by the house and Seán can have the car waiting for you.'

'Come on, so. We don't want to be here too long, and now I know where it is Ned and I can manage. We'll be back tonight to get it ... You're sure they won't bring these rocks in today? Otherwise I won't know which field?'

'Not a chance. I know McDonagh well. He always leaves them out the full week to season, and he won't touch a cock with a spot of dew on it. Says they sweat in the shed! There'll be nobody working these fields before Friday.'

From his hiding-place, Kevin could see the speaker. It was Colm White, the younger brother of a neighbouring farmer, who lived in England now but came home occasionally for a few days. Kevin had seen him earlier that week in Swinford and had given him a wide berth, aware that he was a man known to lose his temper easily.

'You'll meet us in Cork on Sunday as planned then?'

'I will so,' answered Colm. 'The arrangement stands. Good luck.'

'Good luck.'

Kevin tightened his arm around Carrots as he saw one man crossing the field westwards, but luckily he did not look back or he would have seen the boy and his dog. Colm White must have gone back the way he had come as Kevin did not see him again. He remained lying flat until he saw the first man leap over a stone ditch and go striding up the hill beyond, then he slowly raised himself to a sitting position. His heart was still beating fast and Carrots kept licking his face and wagging his tail so hard that it kept bumping Kevin's leg.

'Got it!' hissed a voice behind him, and Kevin jumped in alarm.

'Maureen! You frightened the life out of me! I didn't know it was you!'

'Well, who did you think it was?'

'Don't be dumb. I got a bit of a fright, that's all.'

'What happened? Did a leprechaun pop out of the blackberry bush and ...'

Kevin cut across her. 'I know where the cross is!'

Maureen stared. 'What? Where?'

'There were two men here talking ...'

'And I suppose they told you all about it?'

'... they were on the other side of the fort and they were talking but they couldn't see me. They met here so that Colm White could show the other fellow where the cross was hidden.'

'What's Colm White got to do with it?'

'Don't you see, he's one of the thieves! And he brought one of the gang here to show him where to pick

60

it up because he can't get it himself.'

'Why can't he?'

'Of course I asked him, didn't I? I just stood up and said "Here I am and I've been listening and won't you kindly tell me why you can't collect the cross yourself?" Maybe he just wants someone else to do the dirty work.' He sounded cross.

'Okay, okay, keep your hair on! Where is the cross?'

'Colm hid it under a stone. I expect he thought the guards might be after him and he put it there on the way across to his brother's.'

'Which stone is it under?'

'I didn't see which one he pointed to, but it must be somewhere near the fort. He said something about it slipping down into the wall.'

'Let's have a look, so,' she said, leaning the sickle against the bush and scrambling down the side of the fort again. They set off around the stone wall at the side of the fort and followed it across the headland, but no tell-tale splash of blue was to be seen and it was impossible to tell if any of the stones had been moved recently. To move them was to risk a cave-in as many of the smaller round stones were perched precariously on rubble where walls had fallen and not been rebuilt properly over the centuries.

'What a daft place to hide a cross!' exclaimed Maureen in disgust. 'We're never going to find it! How are they going to know where to look for it? They'll need a metal detector!'

'So daft that no one would think of looking there!' replied Kevin. 'But they know all right! Anyway, one good thing — neither of them was Liam!'

'What did the other man look like?' asked Maureen. 'Maybe he was this fellow Pat that Liam was talking to, the one that's hiding at Dan Moore's.'

'I only saw him from behind. He went off that way, across O'Donnell's fields. He can't be from round here, as he had to have the field pointed out to him.'

'What is he going to do after he collects the cross with, who was it, Ned?'

'They are all to meet up in Cork on Sunday,' said Kevin. 'That must be where they're taking the cross. What do we do now? Go to the police?'

'How can we call the guards in when we don't know which stone it's under? There must be a million stones along the ditches. We can't look under every one — if Dad came out and found all the ditches pulled down he'd half-kill us! And what if we didn't find the cross at all? It's quite small, isn't it! This briefcase it's supposed to be in might be no bigger than a pencil-case ...

'There's only one answer!' she concluded, 'we'll go and tell Teddy now, and the three of us will watch tonight and catch the thieves red-handed. In the meantime, let's go back up to the fort and get that boot!'

Without wasting any time, Maureen climbed back up the fort wall and began to slash away at the larger brambles, and within a few minutes she had cleared a space large enough for Kevin to crawl in and retrieve Teddy's boot. Beneath the branches there was quite a large opening, rather like a small cave, and Kevin made a mental note to come up here and make himself a little hide-out some day. Now that the brambles were cleared from the entrance it would be quite easy for him to squeeze in there with Carrots. Teddy's tree-house was

all very well, but he had to share it with the other two —
and of course Carrot's couldn't climb the tree.

'Have you got it?' called Maureen.

'Yes. And three odd socks as well, and something that
looks like a chewed-up hairbrush! You go on down to
the house while I see if there is anything else!'

'Right you are,' said Maureen, and started off for the
house with the sickle held carefully at right angles to her
body, just as she had seen her father carrying it. She put
it back on its hook in the hayshed and went back to find
the boys.

When she found them, Kevin was already telling
Teddy what he had heard, Carrots was dancing around
the boys barking at full volume, and Teddy was
listening in great excitement.

'Well, what do you think?' asked Maureen. 'I say we
should wait up at the fort tonight and catch the thieves!'

'Don't be an idiot,' said Teddy. 'What chance would
three kids have against two men? You know what they
did to those men from the museum.'

'I think we should tell the guards,' said Kevin.

'I don't think that's a good idea either,' said Teddy.
'What if the police came and the whole thing was a joke?
It might not even be the cross that's hidden there. It
could be a couple of bottles of poteen! Wouldn't we look
the great heroes if we called the Swinford guards out for
that! No, I have a better idea. I'm going over to see Liam
and ask him and his friend to come over. The five of us
together should be able to stop them.'

'How do we know Liam's friend wasn't one of the
men who were talking?' asked Maureen. 'Kevin didn't
see both of them, and we could be getting ourselves into

worse trouble this way. Why don't we tell Dad and let him decide?'

'That's as daft as telling the police,' said Teddy. 'Do you think for one minute that Dad would let us get out of bed in the middle of the night and go catching thieves? We'd miss out on all the fun... and after all, if we're right, we're the ones who solved the mystery.'

'Me,' corrected Kevin. 'I solved it.'

'To be honest,' said Maureen, 'if anyone solved it, it was Carrots. If he hadn't pinched Teddy's boot, none of us would know the cross is hidden here.'

'It's agreed then,' said Teddy. 'I have an appointment to see Liam at eight o'clock tonight and meet his friend. I'll tell him what we're planning then.'

'That's a good idea,' said Kevin. 'Can I come too?'

'No, you can't! Liam said just me and I gave my word. What you can do is get some equipment ready for tonight while I'm at Liam's.'

'What sort of equipment?'

'A couple of torches — and make sure the batteries are good. A big rope to tie the baddies up when we catch them. And you could put a few sandwiches in a bag if you like, then if we have a long wait we won't be hungry! Use one of those flour bags in the press; then it won't rustle when we get the sandwiches out!'.

'Can't you think of anything except your stomach?' groaned Maureen. 'We're off on an adventure and you want to have a picnic! And anyway the sandwiches would be stale by tonight.'

'Just making sure the ranks are working on a full stomach!' grinned Teddy. 'Let's go and have tea, then I'll be off to see Liam. Won't he get a surprise!'

7 *Plans!*

An hour later Teddy was on his bike and off to Moore's. It was fortunate that it was midsummer, so the sun was still shining and he had no need to tell his parents where he was going.

Liam was waiting at the entrance to Dan's lane, a wad of chewing-gum in his mouth. He leaned against the stone pillar, his arms folded and his jaws moving in a circular motion.

'So you weren't afraid to come,' he said. 'I didn't expect to see you. Come on then, I'll introduce you.'

Without waiting for Teddy to answer, Liam led the way across Dan's front field and in behind the hayshed. From somewhere up on the piled hay a glow showed in the gloom of the rafters.

'All clear,' hissed Liam, and then a young fellow, a little older than Liam, slithered down and landed at their feet.

'I told you not to smoke up there,' said Liam. 'You'll set the hay on fire. If you have to smoke, go in one of these sheds.'

Teddy eyed the newcomer with interest. He was powerfully built though rather squat, and he had thick black hair. 'Don't you worry,' he said to Liam in a rather surly voice, 'I'm careful. I don't want a fire any more than you do.'

'Anyway, let's sit down and talk,' said Liam. 'This is Teddy McDonagh, the one I was telling you about. His sister was the one who heard us talking.'

'I still think you shouldn't have brought him here.'

'Look, his sister heard us talking and thought you were tied in with that stolen cross. Do you want her telling that story to the guards? Much better to tell them the truth now.'

'The truth isn't much better.'

'Don't be so stupid, Pat. The truth is, Teddy ... Pat is my cousin.'

Teddy gasped. 'Your cousin?'

'Yes, my cousin. He left his family a couple of years ago, when he was about my age, and got a job on the buildings down in Dublin.'

'Wasn't he too young to be working?' asked Teddy.

'Well, that all depends who you are working for and how tall you are!' laughed Pat sourly.

'Anyway, he got mixed up with some lads who used to break into houses. They got caught and some of them got jail and some got probation. Pat was lucky — he was younger than the others and he got probation.'

'But I'm not supposed to leave the Dublin area,' said Pat. 'I have to stay another six months there and I'm supposed to report in every Tuesday. But I was on the dole and there was nothing to do, no work, and I got so bored. Then I missed the countryside and the freedom of life up here. So I thought, if I could just disappear for a few months, the police might forget about me and I might be able to get a job with a farmer. Something like this job Liam has would be good. That would suit me fine. I heard about Liam being here from some travellers who were down Dublin way, so I headed up here.'

'You walked all the way from Dublin?' Teddy could not believe that.

'It took me a couple of weeks. I had some dole money collected just before I left, and I made it last for food.'

'Where did you sleep?'

'It's summer, isn't it? Anywhere I could. Haysheds, under trees — once I even slept in an abandoned truck. When I got here, Liam hid me on the new hay and he brings me a bag of food each night. I get down after dark and stretch my legs, and I try to spend part of each day sleeping. It's not so bad.'

'It sounds awful,' said Teddy, thinking of his own comfortable farm-house.

'Anyway, you believe me now about the cross?' said Liam. 'Pat had nothing to do with it, no more than I did. We don't even know what it looks like.'

'You will soon!' said Teddy. 'I've got something to tell *you*, now. Just listen to this!' and he began to relate the story of what Kevin had overheard in the fort.

When he had finished, Liam reopened his packet of chewing-gum and offered Teddy a piece. Teddy accepted and sat there in silence as he worked the wad around his mouth. After a couple of minutes' silence, he said, 'Well! It looks like we'll need some help tonight. Will you come, Liam?'

'I wouldn't miss an adventure like that for anything!' Liam's eyes were shining. 'I'll come down before dark and wait for you up in the fort.'

'What about you, Pat?' asked Teddy. 'It would be better if you could come too.'

'I'll have to think about that,' said Pat. 'You know my position. If there's a scuffle and the police catch me, it'll be prison for me. They don't like people skipping probation.'

'There'll be no police,' said Teddy. 'We'll sort them out ourselves. Say you'll come, Pat ... I've got to get back home and let the other two know what's happening.'

'I won't promise,' said Pat. 'Liam will go and I'll make my decision later.'

'All right,' said Teddy. 'I won't push you. See you tonight, Liam!'

'See you,' agreed Liam. 'Good luck!'

When Teddy arrived back home the farmyard was quiet. Kevin and Maureen were in the tree-house and as he passed the corner of the house, wheeling his bike and whistling, Kevin called down to him:

'Hi, Teddy! We're up here! Come on up and tell us what happened.'

Teddy let his bike fall against the trunk of the tree and swung himself up into the branches.

'Where are Mum and Dad?'

'It's okay. They're both in the house. Dad wanted to see the weather forecast. He wants to see if the weather is going to clear up tomorrow. If it turns fine he's going to bring the hay into the shed on Friday. Those thieves were right ... they might lose the cross if they didn't come for it tonight.'

'How did it go with Liam?' asked Maureen. 'At least you've come back in one piece! We thought he might try to kidnap you!'

'Don't be silly!' said Teddy. 'Of course Liam wasn't involved with the robbery. I knew he couldn't be.'

68

'So did I,' boasted Kevin.

'Right,' said Maureen. 'I was the only doubter!'

'Anyway, that other boy was only his cousin Pat!'

'Why were they so secretive, then?' asked Maureen. 'Couldn't he have taken his cousin into Dan's place?'

'Pat is on probation,' explained Teddy. 'He left his family a couple of years ago to work in Dublin and got in trouble with the guards a while ago. He is supposed to stay in the Dublin area until his probation is finished.'

'So that explains the things they were saying about the guards,' said Maureen. 'But if he's on probation why did he leave Dublin? That was a bit stupid, wasn't it?'

'He said he got fed up,' said Teddy. 'I guess he was sick of having nothing to do ... he couldn't get another job and the dole money isn't much. He heard about Liam having work here so he decided to risk coming up and trying to get a farm job for the summer too. But when he arrived in Swinford it was about the same time as the cross was stolen ... and he knew that he would be suspected if the police found him and knew he had been in trouble before. So Liam decided to hide him for a few days until the cross turned up and the real thieves were caught.'

'Didn't he have an alibi for the time the cross was stolen?' asked Maureen.

'He was travelling about a fortnight — he came from Dublin on foot — and nobody would have been able to back him up if he said he was in a certain place. He didn't even sleep in houses at night. He says he spent most nights in people's haysheds!'

'Anyway, the important thing is, Liam is coming

69

tonight, isn't he?' asked Maureen.

'He says he wouldn't miss the excitement for anything. He's going up to the fort before dark, after old
Dan goes to bed. He'll hide up there and wait for us.'

'Is Pat coming too?' asked Kevin.

'He said he's got to think about it,' answered Teddy.
'He's afraid of being recognised if the guards are called
in. Most of the local policemen know him as he used to
travel through the Swinford area regularly when he was
still living with his folks, and if one of them knows he is
supposed to be on probation, he would be in serious
trouble.'

'I wonder if that really is the reason,' said Maureen
suddenly. 'After all, he's been away from his family a
few years now according to you. Wouldn't he have
changed a bit in that time? Maybe the real reason is that
he didn't come straight here from Dublin, as he says,
but came through Westport!'

'That's a silly way to get from Dublin to Swinford,'
said Kevin. 'You'd be going round in circles.'

'Not if there was something you had to do on the
way,' said Maureen. 'Like helping yourself to a valuable
cross? It seems queer that nobody would remember him
on the way up.'

'There you go again! You're too suspicious,' said
Teddy. 'Why would he spend all this time waiting with
Liam if the cross was there all the time? He could have
just taken it and gone.'

'Not if he was on probation,' said Maureen. 'You just
said yourself the police might still recognise him. The
first thing they would do would be to search him — and
that would be the end of the cross. What is more likely is

that he hid it away from Moore's land until his partners could join up with him in Swinford. In the meantime he sent his cousin off riding this way to keep an eye on the field in case Dad decided to bring the hay in early and someone spotted the bag with the cross.'

'That's rubbish,' declared Kevin. 'Colm White was the one keeping his eye on the hay. I told you that before. And if it was Pat, why would he have to wait all that time for his partners?'

'He hasn't a car,' said Maureen triumphantly. 'And maybe they have to wait for that rich American to come over here and collect it.'

'How come you question everything?' asked Teddy. 'Don't you think they would have tried to stop me coming back here tonight if they really were involved?'

'You really are silly,' said Maureen. 'To have kept you there would have made Kevin and me suspect! They know we haven't told anyone else — so all they have to do is collect the cross, then tie us up and leave us like the men in the car. Quite simple!'

'What do you think we should do then?' asked Teddy. 'I still don't think it's a good idea to tell any grown-ups.'

'We could take Carrots. He'd defend us!' offered Kevin.

'You're joking!' said Teddy.

'Hey, wait,' said Maureen. 'I've got an idea. Kevin wouldn't be much good in a scuffle anyway, he's too small. Why don't we post him as sentry out of sight of the fort? Somewhere where he could have a good view of the men collecting the cross? Then he could nip down to the house and collect Dad while Mum goes over to Murtagh's house and phones the guards.'

'That's a good idea anyway,' said Teddy. 'I was a bit worried about the four of us trying to catch two big men. If Liam happens to be on their side as well we'd have no chance at all! This way, if they do get away, we can follow them and the guards will be soon after us.'

'That is, if we're not tied up!' said Maureen sourly. 'Look, I think we'd better get into the house now. It must be after ten o'clock and Mum will start calling us. We don't want too much noise around the farm or it may scare them off. That Colm White could be snooping around still! Kevin, you'd better go straight to bed and pretend to be asleep. I'll be in as soon as I have the ropes and things all ready.'

'I thought you were going to have them all done,' said Teddy.

'We have, but they're still in the shed. I'm going to take them up to the fort now and leave them under that blackberry bush we cut down when Carrots took your boot. If we pile the cut branches back on top, they will be well out of sight.'

Just then the back door opened and the cat trotted out.

'That's Mum, putting the cat out,' said Maureen. 'Go on to bed, Kevin, and you go and keep Mum and Dad talking for five minutes, Teddy, while I go up to the fort.'

One by one they let themselves down from the tree and the boys went into the house quickly. Maureen disappeared up to the back field with a large hessian bag, and a moment later her silhouette could be seen crossing the ridge at the top of the field as the twilight fell.

8 Adventure at Midnight

Eileen McDonagh was surprised how quickly Kevin went to bed. She was about to follow him and ask whether he felt all right when Teddy stopped her by announcing he was going to make some tea.

'Do you think there's anything wrong with Kevin?' she asked him.

'He's tired,' explained Teddy. 'We were doing a lot of running around today with Carrots, after we came back from the bog.'

'So that's why he was so keen to get to bed! I thought he must be coming down with something.'

'He's all right,' said Teddy, adjusting the gas flame under the kettle. 'I'm quite tired myself. Think I'll go to bed as well, just as soon as I've had my tea.'

'Now I've seen it all! Well, another early night won't do any of you much harm. You two big ones haven't been to bed this side of eleven since the holiday started.'

'Is that a teapot I hear?' called a voice from the next room. 'Put my name down for some!'

'I'm making some now, Dad,' called Teddy. 'Be right in with it. You go and sit down, Mum — I'll bring yours in too.'

As his mother went into the little sitting-room to join her husband in front of the television, the back door opened and Maureen arrived, slightly out of breath but smiling.

'I've done it, Teddy. Everything's in place for later

and it's just getting dark now.'

'Good. I'm making some tea, then you and I had better get to bed. Was there any sign of Liam?'

'Nobody around for miles. Not even a dog. It's just as well — I didn't want anyone to see me hiding the bag. It's right under the bush now, and no one would ever see it.'

'I'm going to wear my new watch,' said Teddy, 'then we'll know when to expect them. It glows in the dark so I won't need the torch to check it.'

'We probably won't be able to use the torches anyway,' said Maureen. 'The glow would give us away.'

'You never know,' answered Teddy. 'It's as well to have them just in case.'

'I've put the three in. Kevin's batteries aren't much good but I didn't have any new ones.'

'Oh, we'll manage. Kettle's boiling. Let's get that tea over with, then we can do the decent thing. It must be nearly half-past ten and the old folks won't go to bed until we're all safely tucked in. As soon as we hear Dad snoring it will be safe to move. Whatever you do, don't fall asleep!'

'You must be kidding,' said Maureen, measuring tea-leaves into the pot. 'As if I could possibly drop off! Put that water in here, will you?'

'Did Kevin lock Carrots in?'

'Of course. He did that first, before we got the bag ready. We wouldn't want old Carrots arriving up there and wanting to play with someone's boot!'

'I'm excited,' admitted Teddy. 'I wonder if there really is a reward? Wouldn't it be marvellous if we won a thousand pounds?'

74

'If you stop dreaming, you could get some milk out of the fridge,' said Maureen. 'I thought you were supposed to be in charge of the tea?'

'The milk's already in the cups ... see, smarty? And the sugar too. And here comes the tea. Takes an expert to do the pouring, you know!'

'Is that dad's? O.K. I'll take his in with mine. You bring Mum's and we'll get this evening off to a quick start!'

They went through the narrow doorway to the sitting-room and sat down side by side on the sofa. Teddy, trying to look as though he were not at all impatient, announced, 'I guess I'll be off to bed in a minute, Dad. I'm awfully tired.'

'Good,' said Con McDonagh. 'I won't be too long myself. An early night would do me good, too.'

Teddy tried to hide a smile, and then almost spilled his tea as his father went on, 'Been doing any detective work, Teddy?'

'What sort of detective work?' asked Teddy carefully.

'Oh, you know — that missing cross we were talking about a couple of days ago. You children thought there might be a reward, and said you might do some hunting for it in case it was still in the area.'

'*That* cross?' replied Teddy.

'Oh, we haven't seen anything of it,' said Maureen truthfully. 'I wonder where it could be?'

'Probably halfway to South America,' said Eileen McDonagh. 'I don't suppose the police will ever find it now. The thieves were too clever for them.'

'The guards are pretty clever too,' said Teddy loyally. 'I bet you it will turn up.'

'Let's get out that big Mayo map,' suggested Con McDonagh, 'and see what kind of places they could have made for when they left the community centre. It will do you kids good to do a bit of local geography anyway. The school holidays are far too long! You don't want to go back forgetting everything you were taught last term.'

Teddy looked at Maureen in despair. If their father got the map out he would completely forget that they were all tired and they would spend the next hour on the floor poring over it. Normally the children found this fascinating as Con McDonagh knew almost everything about local history and geography, but tonight was not the night to encourage him to start on his favourite subject! Fortunately their mother came to the rescue.

'Oh, I think we could leave that till tomorrow night, Con. The childen are rather tired tonight. They have had a long hard day at the bog, you know, and they did say they planned on having an early night. Poor old Kevin was so tired he went off without any tea. They are planning on going back to the bog again tomorrow if this weather holds, and then you'll be needing them to bring in the hay. The map can keep until the summer jobs slow down!'

'I suppose you're right. Finish up your tea and get to bed then, kids. We'll have a chat about the map and the cross some other time.'

'I've finished,' said Teddy, standing up and producing a magnificent yawn which made everyone else feel sleepy too! 'Goodnight all.'

'I'm off too,' said Maureen. 'See you all tomorrow.'

She followed Teddy out into the hall and into the

bathroom and the two of them made a great deal of noise cleaning their teeth so that their mother would not arrive down to their bedrooms to see if they had forgotten.

'We leave here at a quarter to midnight,' hissed Teddy through a mouthful of toothpaste. 'Earlier if they get off to sleep quickly. Meet you in the kitchen, but don't turn any lights on.'

'Okay,' said Maureen. 'I'm putting my nightie on over my clothes to save time. Then if Mum comes to see if I'm tucked in, she won't see me asleep in my jeans.'

'Yes, I'll do that too,' said Teddy. 'Which nightie shall I wear?'

'You can't be serious for two minutes at a time!' said Maureen. 'I'm off now. For heaven's sake be quiet when you get up again.'

'I'll be the original mouse,' said Teddy. 'I may have to wake Kevin of course. He said he wouldn't go to sleep but knowing him, he's probably in dreamland already.'

'Lucky him,' said Maureen. 'I guess we'll all be pretty tired by the time this night's over.'

'Don't think about being tired! Think about the adventure we're going to have! Just wait till they hear about this back at school!'

Maureen lay in the dark and watched the clock hands. They were luminous and as the darkness fell the glow strengthened. It was like being back at school — the hands seemed to have weights to hold them whenever she was in a hurry to get outside!

It was hot with her outdoor clothes on but she did not dare creep out from under the blankets in case her mother looked in. One by one, the familiar noises surfaced — the sounds of doors opening and closing, water running, soft voices, the click of a light switch. Once she heard her mother's footsteps in the hall and quickly closed her eyes, but the steps halted outside her door and then she heard a loud whisper, 'They're all asleep. They must have been really worn out!' Then the steps retreated and Maureen dared to open her eyes. Although it was not quite dark she could tell from the faint glow through the curtains and the outline of the various familiar objects in her bedroom that the moon was rising. They would have to take care not to be seen on the hill between the house and the fort. She listened for the sound of her father winding his bedroom clock. That was the signal that he was about to get into bed, and after that the coast would be clear.

She watched the clock hands. Twenty past eleven. She would wait until half past to be sure. It would be disastrous if they were caught leaving the house!

Meanwhile, in the boys' bedroom, Teddy was already out of bed and trying to rouse Kevin without startling him.

'Come on, Kev!' he said softly. 'Time to go. I'll leave you behind if you don't come on!'

The only answer was a slight shrug from Kevin, then he rolled over and tightened his grip on the battered golliwog which still shared his pillow.

'Oh, come on!' hissed Teddy. 'Don't you want to catch the thieves?'

Kevin moaned in his sleep but showed no signs of rousing. In desperation, Teddy tugged at the golliwog and succeeded in pulling it away. That did the trick!

Kevin sat up and opened his mouth ... but Teddy was too quick for him and clapped his hand over it.

'Shut up, you fool,' he said. 'You'll wake Mum and Dad! Don't you want to come on the adventure?'

'Give my golly back first,' said Kevin sulkily, still half-asleep. 'He's mine!'

'Here you are, baby ... now get out of bed, will you? And keep the noise down. Mum and Dad have just gone to bed and if they're not asleep yet they'll hear us and come out to see what's going on.'

Kevin, now wide awake, swung himself out of bed, keen not to be left out of the action!

As quietly as they could, the two boys dressed. Kevin had undressed completely so it took him a few minutes to dress again. Teddy, following Maureen's example, had merely put his pyjama jacket over his outdoor clothes so it took him only a few seconds to get ready.

While Kevin was pulling on his jeans and socks, Teddy heaped the discarded pyjamas under the bedclothes so that anyone looking in at the door would see two humps neatly tucked up and think that the two boys were fast asleep there. This done, they opened the door carefully and padded down the hall to the kitchen. They did not dare to turn a light on, but the faint moonlight shining through from the kitchen door gave them enough light to see where they were going. In the kitchen they put on anoraks and were just pulling on their boots when Maureen appeared.

They did not speak to one another until they were all safely outside the house and had closed the back door. Then Maureen beckoned them towards the tool shed where she had left the torches, and once in the shed with the door closed, she felt free to talk in her normal voice.

'Everything all right?'

'We're early,' said Teddy, 'but that's no harm. I don't think anyone heard us coming.'

'Good. Now, this is the plan. We don't use the torches once we're out of the shed unless it's absolutely necessary. Teddy and I head for the blackberry bush. You,' she turned to Kevin, 'have to be sentry. You know that hawthorn bush on the ditch this side of the fort?'

'Course I do.'

'Well, you can wait there and go off for help as soon as we flash the torch three times. Got that?'

'I've got a better idea,' suggested Kevin. 'Why don't I go up in the tree-house? I'd see more from there and the thieves would never know I was there. I could still see your signal.'

'That's brilliant,' said Teddy. 'He'll have a view of the

whole fort area and some of the Rinn Mór as well.'

'He won't be able to see all the ditches from there,' objected Maureen.

'That doesn't matter,' said Kevin. 'As long as the thieves are somewhere in the field and you can see them, you can send me the signal and I'll go and get Dad to fetch help.'

'That's settled then,' declared Teddy. 'Kevin, you take one torch ... you won't need a rope, will you ? ... and hard luck about the food! Maureen has it all in the fort!'

'No, I left some here in the shed for him. Here you are, Kevin! Cheese sandwiches ... I thought apples would be too noisy.'

'Just one thing,' warned Teddy. 'Don't you go back to sleep or I'll throw your golly away.'

Kevin stuck his tongue out, then switched off his torch and left the shed silently. They watched his shadowy form cross the garden, then round the corner.

'Our turn now,' said Teddy. 'Let's get up to the fort as soon as possible. Liam may be already there.'

'Yes,' agreed Maureen, 'and if he is, we may just need that torch signal sooner that we think!'

However, she followed Teddy's example in making sure her torch was off before the shed door was opened a second time.

Keeping as close to the stone wall as they could, they made their way quickly up the field. Here and there long runners from the ever present blackberry bushes threatened to trip them, but the moon gave them enough light to see by and they managed to reach the fort without stumbling. As they reached the lower fort wall, they stopped and looked back down the field. No one was in sight, and Kevin in his tree-house was completely invisible. The leafy branches had hidden him completely.

'Up here,' said Maureen softly, and led Teddy to the bush where Carrots had taken the boot. 'See, we can creep under those branches and no one will ever see us. It's an ideal hide-out.'

The two children wriggled into the space feet first, pushing the bag to one side. Maureen eased the rope out and pushed it to the entrance.

'Let's leave the sandwiches till later,' she suggested. 'We'll be glad of them if we have a long wait.'

'Liam must have got held up. Maybe Dan hasn't gone to sleep yet.'

'At this hour of the night? Not very likely!'

'Well, he *has* been ill. He could have had a bad turn,' said Teddy defensively.

'He's not sick. It's only a broken ... SSSH!'

Both of them froze as a sudden clattering near the hole broke the stillness of the night. It stopped momentarily, there was a swishing in the hazel branches which hung over the tangle of blackberry, then the scraping sound resumed.

'It's okay, it's only an animal,' hissed Teddy in relief. 'A rat or a weasel, I expect. Listen, you can hear its claws on the stone ditch.'

'Not a weasel!' shuddered Maureen. 'I hope it doesn't live in here!'

'I'd rather have a visit from a weasel than one of the baddies,' exclaimed Teddy. 'I thought you loved animals.'

82

'Like people,' replied Maureen, 'I like some better than others. Liam and that Pat, for example. Liam said he would be here, so where is he? And as for that Pat of yours, he sounds like a trouble-maker. You said he broke probation and came up the country looking for work, so what was he doing sitting on top of the hay smoking? That doesn't sound so trustworthy to me.'

'You didn't meet him,' said Teddy. 'He explained about why he broke probation and why he was hiding. I believe him.'

'That still doesn't explain why he would do a stupid thing like risking the whole hayshed going up in flames. I'll trust the pair of them when I see them here tonight on our side!'

Teddy lapsed into gloomy silence. The nocturnal visitor, whatever it had been, had vanished and the hazel was silent once more. He found himself wondering how long they would have to wait for Liam and Pat, and what they would do if the travellers failed to appear. Kevin would be wondering what was going on, too — Teddy hoped he did not fall asleep and topple out of the tree-house.

'It's a good thing we don't believe in the Little Folk!' said Maureen suddenly. 'Not too many of the old people round here would stay in a fort after dark!'

'What do you mean?' inquired Teddy.

'Uncle Andy used to tell all the old stories when he came to visit us in the winter,' said Maureen. 'I can just hear him telling the tale about this fort. It used to frighten the life out of me when I was little, but of course I'n not afraid now.'

'Of course not,' agreed Teddy, casting a nervous

glance over his shoulder to the interior of the hole.

'He said that his great-uncle decided to dig up the fort once and make it part of the field. It took him a whole day and he was so exhausted after all the hard work he just collapsed into bed and didn't even stop for his tea. He slept through till midnight, and then something woke him up with a jerk. He opened his eyes and there on the rafters was a whole string of glowing lights, turning themselves on and off, and lighting up the room like a fairy cave. He was terrified and just lay there and stared at them, thinking his end had come.'

Teddy felt his skin getting clammy and wished Maureen would stop. Nothing on earth would make him admit that he was afraid, however, so he gritted his teeth as she continued with the tale.

'Next morning he went back up to the fort and guess what had happened?'

'Nothing,' suggested Teddy.

'Nothing my foot! Hadn't the ground been put back exactly as it was the morning before, and every single stone back in its original position? The fairies had not liked him tampering with it, so they had put everything back in its place. No one ever dared to touch the fort again after that, and that is why it has been left here in the middle of the fields.'

'I wish Liam would come,' said Teddy. 'I don't want to wait here all night.'

'I don't expect the fairies will mind us waiting here,' consoled Maureen. 'We'll leave everything exactly as we found it. Stones and all!'

'Maureen! Look!' Teddy pinched her arm suddenly. 'Someone's coming up the field!'

9 Rascal to the Rescue!

Maureen smothered a gasp as she, too, saw the two figures coming round the corner of the McDonagh house. Their shapes stood out clearly against the white-wash of the walls. Several barks announced that Carrots, too, was aware that strangers were on his farm, but as usual all the village dogs immediately began to bark in response so no notice would be taken of the din! The barking subsided as the men reached the centre of the field, then all was quiet once more.

'They're coming!' whispered Teddy. 'Good thing we're down low ... that moonlight is nearly as bright as day. I thought they might come from the direction of the road, and I was right.'

'We can't send a signal to Kevin yet,' Maureen whispered back. 'If I flash the torch now they will see it too.'

'Wait until they pass,' said Teddy. 'Kevin can prob-ably see them from the tree-house anyway, and he cer-tainly will have heard the dogs barking. He'll know we can't signal yet. We'd better be quiet now, they're nearly here!'

The two children crouched close together, barely daring to take a breath. However, the two figures turned away from the stone wall and out into the field, skirting around the bottom of the fort wall. Then they stopped, and one of them appeared to be counting something under his breath as he waved his arm about and surveyed the field. Then the two of them set off down the field among the cocks of hay and as soon as they went Teddy wriggled out from under the bush and, still flat on his belly, made his way to the top of the fort so that he could follow their actions. Meanwhile Maureen aimed her torch towards the house and flashed several times. There was no evidence that Kevin had seen her signal, but the batteries were fresh and the beam was powerful, so she had to assume he would carry out his share of the action. Leaving the torch with the uneaten sandwiches, she looped the coiled rope over one shoulder and began to crawl up the slope after Teddy.

The men had stopped at a ditch near the gate to the back field and now the children could hear them talking softly. There seemed to be some doubt as to which was the right wall, then the taller man's voice was heard with a distinct, 'It's either this one or the one the other side of the gate. We'll have to look under both of them,' and then they started to tear the ditch down and throw the stones to one side. One of them produced a flashlight and directed the beam at the block pier to which the field gate was attached, while the other began to lift the larger flags which formed the foundation of the wall.

In the reflection from the flashlight, Teddy could see that both men wore black balaclavas. He could feel the blood throbbing in his ears so loudly that it threatened to deafen him. He felt he was about to lose control and make a noise. He glanced at Maureen stretched out beside him, but she showed no sign of fear. He desperately wanted to ask what they should do next, but was afraid to open his mouth. Then, feeling his eyes on her, Maureen turned her head slightly and whispered so softly that he could only just make out the words:

'We can't tackle them. Two of us would have no chance at all. Look at the size of the bigger one. We were fools to think we could catch them on our own. We'll just have to wait until Kevin brings help, and hope he is not too late!'

Teddy's relief was unbounded when he heard this. He had been petrified when the reality of what they had planned had struck him. Two youngsters would be no match for two grown men, and he was small for his age which didn't help! If Kevin was quick, they would still be able to take the credit for finding the cross, but leave the work of actually capturing the criminals to grown-ups.

The wall was now completely scattered. It was clear that the cross had not been found, and the smooth face of the pier was exposed to ground level. No hiding-place remained. One of the men grunted as though he was furious with the other, and for a moment the children thought the two were going to have a fight, but then they began moving the stones against the pier on the other side of the gate. Once again pebbles were flung down until the larger flat stones were reached; then they began the slow job of searching the base once more with the aid of the torch.

'They'll find it in a minute and be gone, and there's no sign of help coming!' groaned Maureen. 'They're going to get away with it. We should have told the guards after all!'

What happened next occurred so suddenly and unexpectedly that the children were just as surprised as the thieves. Through the silence of the night there came the unearthly whinny of a pony ridden hard. Then all they could see were the front legs of the animal pawing the sky as she came over the crest of the hill, rearing and snorting and trying to unseat the rider who was spurring her on. The pony came straight at the two men, prancing about and squealing and jerking her legs up before them. One after the other, the two howled with fright and sped towards the fort. Then the rider flung something, a rope came snaking out, and the shorter man was caught fast in a loop which immediately tightened around his shoulders. The pony cantered around him, entwining the rope so that the man was well and truly secured.

'It's Liam on Rascal!' shouted Teddy. 'Quick, the other rope!'

Maureen, guessing what was happening, had already unravelled the rope, and as the tall man scrambled up the side of the fort and collapsed out of breath at the top, the two of them landed on his back in force, causing whatever wind was left in his lungs to explode forth in a deep grunt! Before he could recover, or even work out what was going on, they had wound the rope around his hands and tied them to his feet so that he was powerless. Teddy, however, remained sitting on his back just in case!

With all the excitement of the last few minutes, they had been unaware of anything happening behind them, but suddenly the children realised that not only their father but also four of the neighbouring farmers were standing at the foot of the fort, accompanied by an eager Carrots, all ready for action!

'It's okay, Dad,' called Teddy. 'We've caught the

thieves. The ones that stole the cross. Liam's got one on the end of the rope, and I'm sitting on the other one. There's a man called Seán in a car somewhere down the road, and the fourth member of the gang is Colm White.'

Con McDonagh and two of the men climbed up the slope and the other two went to relieve Liam of his captive.

'Are you all right?' asked Con McDonagh. 'You silly children! These men are dangerous! Why didn't you tell us this was going to happen?'

'We sent Kevin to get you,' pointed out Teddy. 'And none of us is hurt. Don't worry so much!'

'Well, anyway, I suppose you have come out of it all right,' conceded their father. 'Kevin and your mother have gone over to Murtagh's house to phone the guards. They should be here soon. In the meantime, is the cross safe?'

'The cross?' echoed Maureen and Teddy, looking at each other in astonishment. 'We forgot all about it!'

'Then you'd better get down and look for it!' ordered Con McDonagh. 'Go on, before the guards get here. You'll look a bit silly if you haven't any evidence! You could go to jail for assaulting these boyos.' Then, as Teddy hesitated, he added, 'You can get off him, son. I'd say three of us are quite enough to keep an eye on that one!'

The two children raced down the hill towards the tumbled walls, only stopping to collect Maureen's torch. They passed a very well-trussed robber, still sporting his balaclava, and completely under the control of Liam and two burly farmers. Maureen switched on her torch as they reached the second pier.

'They hadn't found it when Rascal chased them,' said Teddy, 'so it must be somewhere near the bottom. You shine the torch and I'll look for it.'

But in the end it was Maureen who found it. While Teddy was lifting a large flag, she saw a flash of colour in the torch beam and exclaimed, 'I've got it! It was right underneath all the stones, leaning against the side of the pier. Look!' and she tugged at the shiny fabric and slid the briefcase out. She unclipped the catch, opened it wide, and closed her fingers round the cross. She lifted it up and the green jewels flashed in the torch beam.

'Those are emeralds,' said Teddy. 'Those shiny green things stuck all the way up. Doesn't look like gold though, does it? You wouldn't think such a dirty little thing could be so valuable.'

'It's because it's so old,' said Maureen. 'It's quite heavy for such a small thing. You feel it!'

Teddy held his hands out and took it from her. The cross was no more than nine inches long, but he had difficulty in holding it steady across one palm.

'You're right, it's heavy. I wonder if it really did belong to St. Patrick once?'

The sound of a car drawing up at the other end of the field alerted them, and they began to make their way back to their father, the cross safely in Teddy's hands. Maureen carried the empty briefcase with great ceremony, goose-stepping a few paces behind Teddy.

'The guards are here,' said Con McDonagh. 'Have you got it? Good! Let's see, Teddy.'

Teddy held it out to him and he whistled. 'Beautiful, isn't it. Look T.P.! Did you ever see a yoke like this?'

The two neighbours examined the cross in turn and nodded.

'Fine piece of work right enough, Con. Your young fellows did a good job tonight!'

'What's going on up there?' came a voice up the field, and three men appeared at the foot of the fort.

'Up here! We have two of the men you're looking for ... and the Westport cross safe and sound!'

The familiar form of Sergeant Sullivan from Swinford appeared on the slope, and then he had scrambled up beside them.

'Well, I see you've done our job for us already! This must be one of the mates of that lad we found acting suspiciously in a car back the road!'

'That's Seán,' explained Teddy. 'He's the driver for

the gang. And the other one is down there with Mr. O'Reilly and Mr. Ryan. Liam has him by the end of the rope!'

Leaving his two men to take charge of the prisoner and the cross, Sergeant Sullivan made his way down the field to where Liam and the two farmers still held their captive tightly. Liam had slipped off Rascal's back but the end of the rope was still attached to her bridle in case the thief tried to escape.

'You've done a good job there, young fellow. Liam O'Connor is it?'

'Yes, sir!' answered Liam nervously.

'Well, now. There's two of my lads coming up the field now to take charge of this one so you can relax. Let's have that balaclava off his face.' Producing a pair of handcuffs, he clicked them in place, then motioned to the farmers to unwind the ropes from the captive's shoulders. As they did so he peeled back the balaclava with one flick of his hand.

Liam turned away, stricken. 'It can't be! You promised! You said you knew nothing about the cross!'

'You shouldn't have interfered,' answered Pat in a sullen voice. 'I told you not to come here this evening with those interfering kids.'

'And you nearly stopped me, didn't you?' said Liam bitterly. 'It was you that gave young Paul Murtagh the message for me. I might have known Dan wouldn't want tobacco that late at night. And I had to go all the way to Swinford and back before I could come over here. No wonder you didn't want me around. You'd only have two kids to deal with!'

'Well, I couldn't stir with you around!' snarled Pat.

92

'Every move I made, there you were breathing down my neck. Can't you see I was doing you a favour, keeping you out of it? It was bad enough having to wait about until Seán's ankle healed.'

'Was he hurt then?' asked Sergeant Sullivan. 'We thought one of you must have been injured. When we interviewed the curator, he told us he had managed to get in a kick at one of you before he was tied up.'

Maureen and Teddy had joined them now, and Teddy stared when he saw who was there, sullen and angry, his hands safely bound.

'You were one of them, Pat! Maureen, Pat was lying . . . he *is* one of the gang.'

'I didn't know,' said Liam, turning anxiously to his friends. 'I believed him too. I trusted him and he lied to me.'

'I'm glad you came tonight,' admitted Maureen. 'Teddy and I were beginning to think you were both involved.'

'Liam saved the day,' said Teddy. 'We wouldn't have caught them at all if it hadn't been for him.'

'Yes,' agreed Sergeant Sullivan sternly, 'although I think we ought to have a little chat with you heroes about mixing yourselves up in police affairs. As it is, we still have the fourth man to locate.'

'You can catch him up in Cork on Sunday,' piped up Kevin, who had just arrived with his mother. 'He's already left Swinford.'

'Hi, sentry!' said Teddy. 'Good job you did there.'

'I went for Dad as soon as I saw the thieves by the house. I see you have the two of them caught.'

'Just one problem,' said Maureen sadly. 'This man

93

here is Liam's cousin Pat.'

Kevin gasped. 'Liam, he wasn't!'

'I know,' said Liam miserably. 'I can't believe it.'

Kevin's lip was trembling. Two big tears hovered in the corners of his eyes, and he gave a loud sniff. 'How could he! How could he be one of the gang!'

'It takes all kinds,' soothed Sergeant Sullivan, patting Kevin's shoulder. 'Hard luck, but it happens.'

'What will happen him now?' asked Teddy.

'On probation? He'll most likely get jail. Maybe that'll teach him to go straight. He's not a bad boy ... family's never been in trouble. He just fell in with a bad lot in Dublin.'

'At least Kevin always believed in Liam,' said Maureen. 'Do you remember, when we thought he might be one of the gang too, you stuck up for him.'

'I knew he couldn't be a thief,' asserted Kevin.

'Friends then?' asked Liam.

'Friends,' agreed Kevin, wiping his face with the back of his hand.

'Can we bring Liam home for some supper?' asked Maureen. 'I don't expect anyone will be able to sleep for a while after all the excitement!'

'Yes,' said her mother. 'If you children get it ready, that is!'

'We've got a rake of cheese sandwiches still in the fort,' offered Teddy. 'I'll go and get them!'

'Good enough, but don't be too long!' warned his father. 'You've all got to be up early in the morning, remember. There's a grand heap of turf to be turned yet!'

Notes for Teachers

In a world of high technology and a slow exodus from the land it is possible that we may come to forget the 'old' way of doing things. The countryside is an important part of our heritage and it would be sad if a new generation of children was to grow up ignorant of the way things used to be done. In *Mystery at Rinn Mór* I have described the making of turf as it is still made in parts of Mayo today, and the cocks of hay standing in the field weathering, just as they have always done. The one house cow is patiently hand-milked, and the bread comes from the kitchen range, not from a supermarket shelf.

The Westport Cross, although itself fictitious, is representative of many archaeological finds brought to light by modern excavations. Westport House is, of course, a major historical building and tourist attraction in West Mayo, and contains many works of art on exhibit to the public.

Suggested projects: A history of turf-making – the different kinds of slanes (local museums should have specimens); haymaking, the old and the new ways – hay vs. sileage; the travellers – their problems, their place in the community; country careers – opportunities for vets and other work linked to the countryside, in forestry and fisheries; archaeological finds in the neighbourhood – discoveries, preservation.

Jo Ann Galligan

Jo Ann Galligan was born in New Zealand, where her first poem was broadcast on local radio when she was six years old. Since then she has written many poems and short stories, some of which have appeared in Connacht newspapers. She has also written several hymns for performance in local churches.

Since 1978, she has lived on a small holding in Mayo with her Irish husband Frank and their three children, David, Cathleen and Helen. She works part-time as a church organist and teacher, and her spare time is spent bee-keeping, rearing poultry, growing vegetables, and writing.

Mystery at Rinn Mór is her first novel, and she is currently working on the sequel.